P9-DWU-065
INSTRUCTORS'
BARRACKS
THE DARKNESS
STORES
THE STABLES
THE DWELLINGS
NURSERY
SLAUGHTER
HOUSE
WHEELWRIGHT

NOMANSLAND

LESLEY HAUGE

NOMANSLAND

HENRY HOLT AND COMPANY

NEW YORK

Henry Holt and Company, LLC
Publishers since 1866
175 Fifth Avenue
New York, New York 10010
www.HenryHoltKids.com

Distributed in Canada by H. B. Fenn and Company Ltd.

Library of Congress Cataloging-in-Publication Data
Hauge, Lesley.
Nomansland / Lesley Hauge.—1st ed.
p. cm.
Summary: Living under a strict code of conduct in an all-female community sometime in the future, a teenaged girl in training for the border patrol discovers forbidden relics from the Time Before.
ISBN 978-0-8050-9064-2
[1. Science fiction. 2. Women—Fiction. 3. Sex role—Fiction.]
I. Title. II. Title: No man's land.
PZ7.H28655No 2010 [Fic]—dc22 2009024152

First edition—2010/Designed by April Ward
Printed in May 2010 in the United States of America by
R.R. Donnelley & Sons Company, Harrisonburg, Virginia

1 3 5 7 9 10 8 6 4 2

For Arild

To the north-east they say there is a great land where the plants aren't very deviational, and the animals and people don't look *deviational, but the women are very tall and strong. They rule the country entirely, and do all the work. They keep their men in cages until they are about twenty-four years old, and then eat them. They also eat shipwrecked sailors. But as no one ever seems to have met anyone who has actually been there and escaped, it's difficult to see how that can be known. Still, there it is—no one has ever come back denying it either.*

—John Wyndham, *The Chrysalids*

NOMANSLAND

CHAPTER ONE

TODAY AMOS, our Instructor, keeps us waiting. Our horses grow impatient, stamping and snorting and tossing their heads. When she does appear, she looks even thinner than usual, her bald head bowed into the wind.

"Tie a knot in your reins," she barks. "And do not touch them again until I tell you."

She has not greeted us and this is the only thing she says. Under her arm she carries a bundle of switches, and our unease is further transmitted to the restless horses. It is some years since our palms last blistered with that sudden stripe of pain, a slash from those slender wooden sticks to help us learn what we must know. We've learned not to transgress in those girlish ways anymore. As we get older, there seem to be other ways to get things wrong, and other punishments.

Amos goes from rider to rider, pulling a switch

from the bundle as she goes, passing each switch through our elbows so that it sits in the crooks of them and lies suspended across our backs. We must balance them thus for the whole of this morning's instruction. For good measure, Amos tells us to remove our feet from the stirrups as well, so that our legs dangle free and we have nothing to secure us to our horses other than our balance.

"You are *my* Novices and you will learn to sit up straight if it is the last thing I teach you." She picks up her own long whip and tells the leader to walk on. We proceed from the yard in single file.

Already the dull pain above my left eye has begun. The anxiety of not knowing what will happen should my switch slip from my clenched elbows, the desperation to get it right, not to get it wrong, throbs in my skull. If we can get away with it, we exchange glances that tell each other our backs have already begun to ache.

The cold has come and the air has turned into icy gauze. In response to the chill wind under his tail, the leader's horse sidles and skitters, then lowers his head. I wonder if he will buck. Today the leader is Laing. Will she be able to stay on if he does buck? What will be the penalty if she falls? Perhaps a barefoot walk across the frosted fields to bring in the brood mares, or being made to clean the tack outdoors with hands wet from the icy water in the trough. At least we are now spared the usual revolting punishment of cleaning the latrines, a task or punishment that falls to other, lesser workers.

But there is nothing to worry about. Laing is also a Novice like me, but she is far more gifted. She's what you might call a natural.

"Concentrate on your center of balance." Amos stands in the middle of the arena and pokes at the sawdust with the handle of her whip, not looking at us as we circle her. From her pocket she takes out her little tin box of tobacco and cigarette papers. With one hand still holding the whip, she uses the other hand to roll the flimsy paper and tamp the tobacco into it. Then she clamps the cigarette between her thin lips.

In my mind I have her fused with tobacco. Her skin is the color of it; she smells of it. I even imagine her bones yellowed by it, and indeed her scrawny frame seems to draw its very sustenance from it. She appears never to have had hair and her eyes are amber, like a cat's. She rarely eats, just smokes her cigarettes one after the other. Where does she get the illicit tobacco from? And the papers? And from where does she get the courage to do something so disobedient so openly? It is a mystery, but a mystery that we would never dare question. And the little painted tin box in which she keeps her tobacco is another mystery. It is a found object from the Time Before, made by the Old

People, who were not like us. "Altoids," it says on the lid. None of us knows what it means.

Amos has had to drop the whip in order to light the cigarette, but it's swiftly back in her hand. She sends a lazy flick, the lash moving serpentlike across the sawdust to sting the hocks of my horse.

How does a serpent move? I am not supposed to know because we have never seen such a thing in our land. They do not exist here.

And yet I do know. I know because I read forbidden pages and I saw a forbidden image upon those pages. I saw the creature entwined in the branches of a tree. And I read the words: *Now the serpent was more subtil than any beast of the field which the LORD God had made. And he said unto the woman, Yea, hath God said, Ye shall not eat of every tree of the garden?*

When I handed those pages back, the Librarian turned white with worry at what she had done, for it was she who had mistakenly given me those pages. But this is how I know things. I know a great deal because I am one of the few who likes to read the pages. There are piles upon piles, all stored, as if they were living things, in wire cages in the Library. No one really likes it that I visit the Library so often, but then there is no real rule that forbids it either. I knew never to tell anyone I had read something not meant for my eyes. I think we are all getting better at keeping secrets. I should be careful what I think about in case it somehow shows.

Amos must have seen me watching her. "Trot on," she says. "You look like a sack of potatoes." Again her whip stings my horse and he lurches forward, but she says nothing more, only narrowing her eyes through her own smoke as my horse blunders into the others, who have not speeded up. For a moment there is clumsy confusion as some of the horses muddle about and her silence tells us how stupid we all are, particularly me.

Amos was once one of the best Trackers we have ever had. From her we will learn how to use our crossbows, how to aim from the back of a galloping horse, to turn the animal with just the merest shift of one's weight. We are getting closer and closer to what will eventually be our real work as Trackers: guarding the borders of our Foundland, assassinating the enemy so that they might not enter and contaminate us. We are women alone upon an island and we have been this way for hundreds of years, ever since the devastation brought about by Tribulation. There are no men in our territory. They are gone. They either died out after Tribulation or they just moved on to parts unknown. As for those who live beyond our borders, the mutants and the deviants, the men who might try to return, we do not allow them in. No man may defile us or enter our community. We fend for ourselves. There are no deviants or mutants among us. No soiled people live here. We are an island of purity and purpose. We must atone for the sins of the people from the Time Before—they who brought about Tribulation.

Our future duties as Trackers seem a lifetime away. For now there is just this: the need to keep my back straight, the need to keep my horse moving forward.

BY THE TIME we get into the tack room to finish the day's cleaning, it has started to snow properly. The horses are all in for the day, brushed down and dozing, waiting for their feed.

The tack room is one of my favorite places. It is a long, low building made of mud and wattle, with a thatched roof and a floor made of yellow pine planks that must have been pulled from some pile of found objects made by the Old People, before Tribulation. Their surface is so smooth, so shiny, not like the rough surfaces we live with most of the time.

The room smells of saddle soap and I love to look at the rows of gleaming saddles and bridles on their pegs. They are precious things. I run my hand over the leather, making sure that no one sees me doing this. Sensuality is one of the Seven Pitfalls: Reflection, Decoration, Coquetry, Triviality, Vivacity, Compliance, and Sensuality. It is, we are told, a system to keep us from the worst in ourselves, and has been thought out by all the leaders of the Committee over all the years we have been forging our lives.

The trouble is that these things are so devilishly hard to watch out for, or even to separate from one another ("which is why they are called Pitfalls," says Parsons, one of the Housekeepers).

Outside the snow flurries and whirls with its own silent energy, and I catch sight of my face in the darkening window. Reflection: I have fallen into two Pitfalls in as many minutes. Nonetheless I stare at it, my eyes large and frightened in this defiance; the broad nose and the wide mouth; my face framed by my wild, coarse black hair, cut to regulation length. I am one of the few whose hair still grows thick.

The Prefect in charge has pulled up a stool in front of the stove in the corner, although she keeps turning to look in my direction.

"Keller!" But she doesn't bother to move from her cozy spot.

I drop my gaze to my work, rinsing the metal bits in a bucket of water, which is cold and disgusting now with the greenish scum of horse saliva and strands of floating grass.

The door opens and some of the snow blows in. Laing comes in too, stamping the snow off her boots. She is carrying a saddle, which she loads onto its peg.

Laing is, and no other word suffices, beautiful. We

are not allowed to say these things, of course, but everyone knows it. She has a sheaf of silver-blond hair, albeit only regulation length, but even more abundant than mine. She is, if anything, slightly taller than I am. Although her complexion is pale, she has surprising black eyebrows and eyelashes that frame eyes so dark blue that in certain light they almost seem violet. Her carriage indicates the way she is, haughty and rather full of herself. She takes a moment to stare, both at me and the mess in the bucket, and says, "You should get some clean water."

"I'm almost done," I answer, but she is already walking away. "Laing, do you want to wait up and then we can walk back to the Dwellings together?" I don't know why I suggest this. Although she is in my Patrol, I would not exactly call Laing my friend. We are not allowed friends, anyway.

She stops and turns quite slowly, quite deliberately, and says with what I can only say is some peculiar mixture of determination and exultation, "My name is not Laing." She hesitates for only a moment and then hisses, "It is Brandi."

Glancing back to make sure the Prefect does not see us, she advances toward the window, which is now steamed up with condensation. She catches my eye and begins to write the word BRANDI on the windowpane.

It is all I can do not to gasp at the sin of it, the forbidden *i* or *y* endings to our names and indeed the very falsehood of it. There's no way in hell she could be called that name. But there it is, written for all to see, in trickling letters on the windowpane. I am so shocked that I do not even move to rub it out, surely the prudent thing to do. But she knows how far she can go, and before I can move, she sweeps her hand over the forbidden name, leaving nothing more than a wet arc on the steamy surface. She turns and suddenly smiles at me and puts her finger to her lips.

"Our secret," she says. "I'll meet you outside when you've finished."

I look quickly at the mark in the window where she wrote the name, willing it to steam back up again. If the Prefect asks what we were doing, messing about back here, I will be hard put to make up anything.

After drying and polishing the remaining few bits and buckling them back into the bridles, my heart is pounding and my fingers do not work as fast as they should. The throbbing above my left eye, which had eased, returns.

For there was something else that Laing had displayed, not just the peculiar, transgressive name marked on the window, but something I couldn't even place or classify. When she wrote the name on the window, I saw something completely new to me.

There, on her finger, was an extremely long, single curved fingernail painted a shade of dark pink that somehow also sparkled with gold. When she held her finger to her lips, it was that finger she showed me, the nail like some kind of polished, spangled talon.

I have never seen anything like it.

CHAPTER TWO

THE WEARYING RIDE, my throbbing head, and the worry about Laing's inexplicable (and stupid) behavior in the tack room have exhausted me. But before I can sleep I have to endure Inspection, which is always a dreary, pointless affair.

Every night the Prefects come into our Dormitory, and the first thing they do is fill in the menstruation charts and allocate sanitary belts and napkins to those who need them. If more than three of us are cycling together, the Headmistress must be notified, for that could mean a fertility wave is in progress and the Committee Members from Johns, the place from which we are governed, must be sent for in order to commence impregnation. But this hardly ever happens to us. I don't even know why they log *our* cycles, since the Patrol is almost always spared. We are too important because we are meant to guard the borders, not to breed. Still, they like to know our cycles. They like to know everything.

The Prefects carry out a number of mostly petty duties. I can't say that I respect them in the same way I would respect an Instructor, but you have to do as they say. They monitor our behavior and report everything to the Headmistress. And they administer many of the punishments.

When the Prefects are not breathing down our necks (and when they are not breathing down the necks of the Novices and Apprentices in the other Orders—Seamstresses, Nurses, and so forth), they do have another duty. They are supposed to search for found objects from the Time Before. But those finds are so rare now that they have almost ceased searching for them, which means they have even more time to pester us, such as now, at Inspection.

Tonight, as every night, they check us for general cleanliness and they inspect our hands and feet. The other thing they do, which they seem to enjoy the most, is make sure no fads have arisen. It is the Prefects' duty to "nip them in the bud," as they like to say.

A few weeks ago there was a fad for pushing up the sleeves of your jacket to just below your elbow, and there is one that is gaining popularity, which is to bite your lips hard and pinch your own cheeks to make the skin bright red. Well, that one comes and goes quite regularly because it is harder for the Prefects to spot.

There are so many rules. Whatever we do, whether we overstep or stay within the lines, we are kept in a perpetual dance of uncertainty in these matters.

Tonight the Dormitory is particularly cold and we want to get into bed. Three Prefects, Proctor, Bayles, and Ross from the tack room, march into the Dormitory, flapping the menstruation charts and taking out their tape measures. Tonight they are checking to make sure our hair has not exceeded regulation length. They do this every so often when they suspect that those who have thick hair have let it grow beyond shoulder-length. Long hair is a dreadful vanity, they say, falling somewhere in the Pitfalls between Reflection and Triviality.

Proctor is still fussing with her chart as Bayles starts to make her way down the line with her tape measure. Bayles is taller than the average Prefect but is still shorter than I am. She is heavily built, has hair like wheat stubble, and she has to wear thick eyeglasses. She yaws at me with her buckteeth and her eyes are grotesquely magnified behind the lenses of her ugly eyeglasses. The Nurses must have supplied her with them from some store of found objects; I do not think we have figured out how to make that kind of glass.

I dread the moment when Laing will be required to show her hands. Is that pink claw still there? I don't know how to explain it. Where did she get it?

Bayles takes up a position in front of Laing, her stubby legs planted far apart, staring at her, but Laing just looks over her head as if Bayles were not there.

"You have let your hair grow past the regulation length again," says Bayles. "You are vain." She waits for a response but there is none. "You think you are someone special, don't you?"

Laing still refuses to look at her.

"You will rise half an hour earlier and come down and have one of the Housekeepers cut your hair." Bayles takes a handful of it and yanks Laing's head back. "It's a good inch too long," she snaps. She peers into Laing's face. "I could tell them to cut the lot off." Her eyes swim and roll about behind the thick lenses as she glares at me because I am craning forward. She turns her attention back to Laing. "Feet," she says and looks down. Our feet, which are bare, have turned blue. "Hands."

Laing holds out her hands, palms facing up. Again I turn my head in her direction as far as I can without being noticed. "Other way," says Bayles, and Laing turns her hands over. "Proctor," says Bayles, "come and look at this."

Both Proctor and Ross, who have heard that dangerous "aha" note in Bayles's voice, come hurrying over and together all three of them pore over one of Laing's fingernails.

"What is that white line?" asks Proctor. "Here,

this line here, by the cuticle." Proctor has pincered the offending finger between her own thumb and forefinger, and her brow is furrowed as she bends over Laing's hand. Bayles and Ross have swelled with the importance of the discovery, their expressions a mixture of bossy importance and sheer delight. "What is it?" says Proctor again.

Laing sighs as if she were bored and tries to reclaim her finger from Proctor's grasp. For an instant they tug back and forth but in the end Proctor lets go.

There is silence and we all wait in the chill, tense atmosphere.

Laing looks over the Prefects' heads again and down the line at all of us. Unbelievably, she winks at me. A ripple of apprehension runs down the line. She splays her hand again, inspecting her nails herself, tilting them this way and that. And then she yawns.

Proctor reddens with anger. "What is that stuff on your fingernail?"

"Glue," says Laing.

Proctor blinks stupidly at her. "Glue?"

"After supper, I was helping the Housekeepers paste coupons into their ration books. I guess I just didn't wash it all off."

Proctor takes the finger again. With her own finger, she picks at the offending line of white stuff. It is indeed resinous and sticky.

When at last they leave, we are free to snuff out the oil lamps and fall into bed. The wind howls outside, and the snow must now be piling in drifts against the walls and the fences we have built to protect our lands and to keep things in order.

CHAPTER THREE

THE SNOWSTORM has so far shown no sign of letting up, but we continue as normal with our training and chores. Chores are so very, very boring. I try to get them done so that I can get to the Library. One or two of the Housekeepers have taught some of us how to read, but we have not learned to read well. I suppose reading is not a useful thing and yet there is so much in those pages! In the free hour, the precious free hour, before Inspection when the others are playing darts or chess, I read whatever I am allowed. I read about the life cycle of something called a guinea worm, explanations about planets and doorknobs and the pigmentation in a pink bird from long ago called a flamingo, how glass is made, and the rules of an idiotic game called croquet. There is much to learn, and yet there is almost nothing about the Old People from the Time Before. It is best that we learn as little as possible about those sinners. I thought at first that perhaps the Old People were not allowed to write about themselves too often, but then one day a Librarian said, "They remove the pages about the Old People. They take them to *her* private Library, in Johns. There are some things we do not need to know."

What are the things we do not need to know? And who is *she*? They won't tell me.

The pages containing graven images have been destroyed, although sometimes an image slips by on one of the pages that you can read. I do look at them. You can't blame me for being curious.

I suppose you could say the Dwellings in which we live provide our biggest clue to what it might have been like in the Time Before. There is a stone archway at the entrance to the Quadrangle, and you can see the words SAINT HILDA'S COLLEGE FOR WOMEN etched into its crumbling surface. We don't know what they mean.

The main building is huge and made of hewn stone. Near the Dwellings and the Stables, there are a couple of other rather dull buildings, grayish and rectangular with no windows. They are protected by a high fence and some rolls of barbed wire, also left over from the Time Before. These buildings are stores for found objects that may or may not be toxic; we cannot use them until the Headmistress has deemed them proper. Beyond those buildings, also surrounded by razor wire, are some more boxlike, metal structures, which is the Darkness, where, after grave error, miscreants must go in order to contemplate and reclaim their purity. Sometimes they don't emerge from the Darkness. They just vanish, as if they had never been among us at all.

THIS MORNING we went snowshoeing for the first time since this cold spell arrived. We went a good fifteen miles in silence and snow, the ice flakes whipping into our eyes so that in the end I closed mine and carried on blind. At least I did not have one of my headaches. I know they are a terrible weakness of mine. Women with headaches—the Instructors hate to hear of such things.

We had started out at dawn, which was marked by a single crimson line on the horizon that slipped away almost immediately, leaving a leaden sky full of snow. Laing had risen even earlier to have her hair cut, ghosting through the dark Dormitory. I woke too but before I drifted back to a few more moments of warmth and sleep, I noticed Carrow getting up and following her. Carrow is in no need of a haircut for she already has short hair. Why would she be going downstairs to the cold kitchen at this hour? If they are being "friends," then that is disobedient, disloyal to the whole.

And yet what is it to be a friend? What do you have to do, or to be, to get a friend?

I want one.

We are to spend the remainder of the day in the Armory, where we keep our weapons. We strip, clean, and reassemble the rifles, and outside the snow falls thickly as we toil away at our greasy, complicated work. Amos moves from one to the next, timing us with her stopwatch, cigarette at the corner of her mouth, tipping back her head and expelling the smoke through her nostrils like a skinny little dragon. There has been no more talk of sticky fingernails, so Laing's story must have held.

The Armory is in the annex, near the east wing of the main College building. It is a gloomy place to be, with little more than slits in the wall to let in the light. The ammunition is kept in great locked wooden chests and only Amos has the key. But when I can, I love to shoot, to hold the weapons against my body and in my hands. Breathe in, breathe out a little but not all the way, hold steady, and fire.

As the afternoon wears on, the Armory grows even darker and Amos lights a few more lamps. The air becomes fatty with the smell of the smoking tallow. Laing and Carrow have been together all day. We have had little opportunity for talking, so they can't have said much to each other. There was definitely the odd giggle. Giggling infuriates everyone and is forbidden, under Vivacity, but like all the Pitfalls, it happens in one way or another. "Giggly little girls," snaps Amos if she hears it. "Pathetic giggly girls."

I do wonder about Carrow from time to time. She has very fine, pale red hair that lies close to her head, pale eyelashes, and skin so white there is something almost indecent about it. She's not what you could ever call a mutant, but she isn't quite normal either. There are almost no mutants now. It has been years since any calf was born with two heads or the plague of barren, eyeless chickens that once troubled our outlying farms. The girl-children at the Nursery are all perfect too.

Laing leans in close to Carrow and says something that I cannot hear. Carrow nods meaningfully in my direction and narrows her eyes at me. I have no idea what they are talking about, so I turn away and try to think about something else.

I have finished before the others, which is never a good thing and means I will doubtless be given something more to do—which indeed I am. I am to go to the Wheelwright and collect the new bows. Ordinarily this would be something I would look forward to because, if I have any friend in the world, it is Smith, who was once a Tracker and is now the Wheelwright.

But today, after the long, blind snowshoeing trek and the sniggering "best friends" in the Armory, all I want to do is go back to the Dwellings, eat, get through Inspection, and fall asleep.

At least this trudge through the snow is easier than I thought. There must have been sledges passing this way because I can walk in the tracks left behind. To the east, a gold moon is rising over the mountains and the quiet is absolute. There is a sense of surcease in the dwindling snowflakes and the failing light.

Transported by the sudden beauty of the moon and the sky, at first I cannot place the sound of bells as a couple of dog sleds race toward me. In the drawing darkness they look just like a pack of wolves, their faces flecked with saliva, black lips pulled back from their teeth as they strain under the whip. I misjudge how fast they are going and they are upon me far more quickly than I thought. I have to jump aside, press myself against a snow-covered boulder to let them pass. There are three people in each sled: a driver and, I see now, two Committee Members apiece. I only glimpse them as they pass, but long enough to see their furs, seal and beaver, mink and silver fox. They turn their heads but barely look at me, anxious to get to their destination before real darkness descends. Their faces are hardly visible under their fur hats and wraps. One of them wears something strapped over her eyes, a kind of band of yellow glass. Perhaps it is this special eye mask and the way she holds herself that makes me think she is their leader.

There is a cry and crack of the whip from the driver and they disappear from view as quickly as they had appeared, leaving crisp furrows in the snow where the runners have been. I stare after them, shivering with something besides cold.

Why have they come? If they have not come to inspect or rebuke us, then there is only one other reason why they are here. There have been no Shearings, no Silent Beatings, no Cleansing Circles as far back as I can remember. The Headmistress and our Instructors keep order in all that we do and we have no recourse to the Committee, except for one thing that only they can do. The thought of what they may be bringing with them makes me feel heavy with apprehension.

Please, not that. Not us. Not now.

Even before I reach the outer workshop I can see the gusting clouds of steam, behind which I can hear some of the Apprentices yelling and hammering. The bulky form that is Smith, the Wheelwright, steps out from the steam carrying a can of water. She wipes her face with the back of her arm and then smiles when she sees me. Behind her the wheel with its new hoop of freshly cooled iron hisses and sizzles, and she turns her attention back to it, pouring on a little more water and watching the puffs of steam thoughtfully. Making a wheel is a process of tiny questions and answers, judgment and alteration that an untrained eye cannot fully acknowledge.

When I come closer, a hint of a shadow flits

through her eyes, if only for a second, before she says, "You up early this morning?"

Her voice is so kind. She must have seen how tired I am, and although it is all she says, I feel a kind of weakening of the soul and almost lose my balance, as though I might at any moment fall into her arms and sob. Embarrassed at the knowledge that she has witnessed me in my moment of weakness, I say rather stiffly, "I have to get the new bows. Amos sent me."

"Well, they're ready. But I'm stopping for tea and so are you," she says, and grins again. She leads the way to the inner workshop, which is packed with timber as well as all the piles of curved felloes and unfinished wheels scattered around like spiky wooden stars. Beyond is the roaring furnace that Smith shares with the Farrier. I have always thought it a wonderful place to be.

Smith has two peculiar leather chairs set by a small iron stove. The chairs, which are found objects, must have been a reward for all her years of service and hard work. They are shabby and pouched from all the years of use, but comfortable, so unlike the little wooden stools that we are accustomed to. More interesting still is that there is a remarkable device on each of them. When you lean back, an attached portion rises to support your feet. Once, while inspecting these mechanisms, I saw a word printed somewhere underneath. *Stressless,* it said, and then *HomeWorld*

Furniture. There were some other numbers and letters that had faded; I could only make out *street* and *California*. They are words that mean nothing to us.

"How is Amos? I haven't seen her for some time." Smith has settled her bulk into one of the chairs and I sit down in the other. Smith and Amos have some kind of liking for each other that baffles me, the one so open and easy in her manner and the other so impenetrable.

"She is the same. We never seem to please her."

"Pleasing her is not what you are supposed to be doing." Somehow when Smith says things like that it sounds reasonable, as if it is something to think over, not another rule to torment us. "You won't get a better Instructor, you know. She isn't easy to read, I grant you that. But I can tell you, she knows you inside out. And you matter to her very much."

"She has a funny way of showing it."

And Smith laughs, a laugh rich with phlegm that turns into a hacking cough. Away from the workshop, she is a smoker too.

"On the way here I saw two sleds carrying Committee Members."

Smith stops laughing. "Where were they headed?"

"Toward the Dwellings, I think. They were using the dogs that they keep at Bareneed Farm, so I guess they will be taking them back there afterward."

Smith swigs the last of her tea, then leans forward to hold her scarred hands out to warm over the belly of the stove. "Carrying Seed, I expect." And she looks at me, her expression both sad and reassuring at once.

"There must be a fertility wave in progress," she says. And then in a whisper, almost to herself, she adds, "We are so few now, we are . . ."

Perhaps she has heard my heart beating, because she does not finish her sentence. For sure she sees the fear in my eyes. "Not you," she says softly. "Not yet, if ever. I bet it's the Seamstresses or the Nurses, or even the Prefects." She smiles but it is not a real smile. "It is our duty," she says, but without much heart.

I grip my empty cup and will myself not to show any more fear or weakness.

"I'm too young," I say. "We are too young, all the Patrol." My voice betrays me. "And they don't choose Trackers. Not often, anyway."

I try to think back to the sled packed with their furs; the cold, pale faces; the leader with the band of yellow glass over her eyes; and the wolf-dogs flashing by, spraying snow from their skidding paws. I try to recall if I saw the frozen metal carrier that contains the Seed or the implements in the black bag. But they sped by so fast and the light was weak.

Smith levers herself out of the chair and holds out her hand to me.

"Back to work." With ease she almost lifts me

from the other chair. She pulls me toward her and tucks a stray lock of my hair behind my ear. As we go out into the yard, she stops and contemplates the hoop of iron that she was cooling earlier. The yard is empty now. The Apprentices have all gone indoors to eat supper. The furnace still glows red and the snow seems to bring extra peace to the quiet yard.

"Tell me, Keller," Smith says, "I often wonder about something." She seems momentarily lost within herself as she looks up at the first stars beginning to show in the darkening sky. "Do you think a woman invented the wheel?"

It is the strangest question I have ever been asked.

THERE IS no light in the Refectory windows when I make my way up the driveway to the Dwellings, which means I have missed supper. I go around the back and come in through the kitchens.

"I kept a pan of stew warm for you," mutters Parsons, trying halfheartedly to conceal her act of kindness from the other Housekeepers. She knows how hungry we get.

"Where have you been?" She is scrubbing the big wooden table in the middle of the kitchen. There is a boiled quality to Parsons with her thickened, mottled skin and raw bones, but she, like Smith, is always one of the kind ones. We know who they are.

"I was sent to the Wheelwright on an errand."

"Some Committee Members came by. The Chair herself is with them, apparently," she says. She turns her gaze and stares out into the darkness, as if they might suddenly rear up at us in the window. When she looks at me again, her face is racked with worry. "Hurry up and take off your things. I'll get your food. There was apple pie," she adds, "but they fell on it like starvelings."

"Why is the Committee here?"

It's a question I don't really want answered. We all know that only the Committee Members can inseminate, and we know too how harshly they inflict the laws of the land.

"I don't think they're carrying Seed," she murmurs. "No one saw the carrier or the implements." She pushes the pan of stew nearer to my bowl, gesturing for me to finish the last of it. "What of the menstruation charts?" Since it is one of their few important duties, the Prefects are fierce about guarding the charts.

"I think there are two of us who are together and the rest are cycling at separate times."

Parsons slumps back in her chair. "I don't think that's a fertility wave, then."

"They don't do us. We're too important." I sound so sure, so certain. "They can't waste us."

It is a big risk to say such a thing but Parsons just looks back at me and says bleakly, "I think it depends."

But on what, she does not say. Instead she says that it's time for me to take a bath.

The Bath House is perhaps the most peculiar of our buildings, not least because of some of the images in there. Unlike the ugly pit latrines, the Bath House is quite a beautiful place, although much has been scraped away so that we will not be contaminated by Decoration. But even so, I love to take my bath.

There is a big room, like a hall, with a big tiled pit in the floor that, I think, was once filled with water for swimming. There are smaller rooms for washing, with drains in the floor, and the walls and the floors are tiled in blue and green. There are spaces where things have been ripped out—a series of objects that must have been long and rectangular and fastened to the wall. I did ask Parsons about those and she said they would have been looking glasses, which are forbidden. "There is no point in looking upon your own image, is there?" she said and added, as if I did not already know, "Reflection is a Pitfall. It leads to vanity and the emptiness of self-love."

They have not made such a good job of removing the images, because here and there are traces of the ones we think the most fascinating: the women with hair at least four times longer than regulation length—and they are bare-breasted! How gentle their sun must be! The most surprising thing is that they have no legs, but instead have tails like fish that make them look somehow passive and hampered and useless. I suppose they could swim well, but they are lying about on rocks doing absolutely nothing. What lives they must have lived in the Time Before, lying idle upon their smooth surfaces under their warm sun.

Everyone talks a lot in the Bath House because somehow the walls distort our voices into echoes. In there, we think ourselves loud and free. And then there is the shuddering delight of sluicing ourselves with the buckets of hot water—all so very different from the Cleansing Circle, which fills my heart with dread.

When I get there, the others are almost finished. They are subdued, toweling themselves dry and not saying very much. In their nakedness they seem smaller and thinner, and after the scrubbing, their skin is pink, like the girl-children we sometimes see when the Moms lay them down on blankets on the grass to kick and squirm during the rare spells of warm weather.

I don't want to think about our bodies, our legs splayed and strapped up like slain beasts as the Committee Members probe with their implements, driving the Seed inward, the Seed that will make us slow and useless and distended with a pregnancy. Our breasts will fill with milk, grow heavy and blue-veined, and then, when it is time, there will come the ripping, the splitting, and all the horror of repeated childbirth if you turn out to be a Breeder. If you dare to give birth to a boy-child, they will take it away, abandon it, and your birthing agonies will have been for nothing.

The facts of life.

I will run away rather than submit to impregnation.

"I saw them," I say. "On the way to the Wheelwright, I saw the Committee Members but I didn't see any Seed carrier. I didn't see the black bag of implements. And we have no fertility wave among us. They're not here for us. It must be for another reason. Or perhaps there is a fertility wave among another group." I sound so authoritative.

"Where were they going?" Carrow is wearing only her woolen pants and socks. Her torso, like one of the fish-women, is bare. She is as strong and tall as the rest of us but when I look at her, I notice how the bones of her shoulders seem suddenly fragile, as if they could be snapped like twigs. Her small breasts and nipples are even paler than the rest of her, the skin almost translucent, a mere membrane, so that to touch it would be to almost touch the very insides of her.

"They were coming from Bareneed Farm. They looked to be coming in this direction."

I don't have the heart to tell them that they have

already arrived. I lift the bucket and pour the water over my head, letting it cascade down my body, shutting my eyes and allowing myself to experience nothing else, nothing at all except warm water and darkness.

The others watch me, waiting for more information, more reassurance. I open my eyes.

"They don't impregnate Trackers," I say finally. "They need us too much."

CHAPTER FOUR

A LINE of geese lifts and flies toward the cold hills. I can hear the beat of their wings as they pass overhead. Late in the afternoon Amos ordered me to shoot a stallion, an ancient, ribby chestnut with hollow flanks who had become useless to us. Amos started asking me to shoot the useless animals some time ago. I sensed that she liked to watch me struggle to get a grip upon my feelings whenever I held the gun to the tethered animal. I no longer allow her that pleasure. I have learned to hide what I am feeling and, in truth, that struggle within is not so hard now.

The stallion's blood covers my boots and I need to get the big winch so that he can be lifted and wheeled over to the slaughterhouse. There will be stallion stew for supper for quite some time. After the noise of the gunshot there seems to be an even deeper silence. The stable yard is deserted until I see Laing, who, as far as I know, should be in the Armory.

She crosses the yard and falls into step beside me tossing her hair, which is her latest fad. It is only a matter of days before the Prefects put a stop to it. She runs her hands through it to further disarrange it. The late-afternoon light, stretched now in a ragged line over the hills, conspires to further the effect by glowing upon the tresses that have arranged themselves just so. Although she cannot possibly see herself, she still seems to know that this effect is there.

"I thought you were supposed to be in the Armory."

"I finished early. There were only Prefects supervising us, anyway. I told them that Amos had sent for me to help you with the slaughtered horse."

"So have you come to tell me what you are up to? What is all this secret stuff about?"

I mean to sound challenging but I think she sees right through me.

"I hear they are leaving tomorrow," she says.

"Who? Who is leaving?"

"The Committee Members. They are going to take horses and ride back to Johns. They can't take the sleds now because of the thaw. A big thaw is coming. Warmth! Yippee!" She skips a few paces and flings her arms up in the air, capering about the stable yard. "The sun. The real sun! Even if it is just for a few days before another snowfall. I'm going to strip off and sunbathe."

I don't know what she is talking about. Sunbathe? Strip off? The only place we are allowed to take off our clothes is in the Bath House. I frown and stomp along without comment.

"You're so serious," she says, dragging the word out as though it were costing her to utter it. She adds one of her little pink cat yawns, as if there were nothing more boring in the world than me. She is still prancing about, singing to herself under her breath, temporarily forgetting to toss her hair. Perhaps I should remind her: *Isn't it about time for a hair toss, Laing?*

Before I can say anything, she starts up again, this time putting her arm around my shoulders. The contact surprises me and I flinch, then tense up. Still, she does not remove her arm. I look around, anxious in case a Prefect or an Instructor should appear, but only the horses waiting for their feed are watching us.

"They never came to impregnate us at all," she says. "I know what they really came for. I even know where it is." She skips away again. I wish she would just walk beside me instead of dancing about. We should not dance.

"The thing is, they don't know where to look," she says, her voice lower now, and more urgent. She has stopped dancing and seems to have forgotten altogether about tossing her hair or prancing about, but her eyes are shining.

"And you do?" I wonder if she hears the tremor in my voice.

"Yes," she says. "I know where to look. And the reason I know where to look is that I found it first."

"And I take it you have not told the Prefects?" This is a stupid question but my mind is racing.

"No." She delivers this with some contempt. "Do you think me completely insane?"

"How did the Committee Members hear of it?"

"They have maps from the Time Before. Secret maps that only Committee Members may look at. That's why they are always in that Library. They are conducting surveillance of the outlying lands."

I am seized by a dangerous curiosity. "So what is it? What's there?"

"I'll show you," she says and again sweeps an arm through the weight of her silver hair. She stands serenely as her hair floats to rest once again upon her shoulders. At this moment she seems capable of anything. "Tonight," she says and touches my arm. "I'll wake you."

SHE WAKES me at around midnight and tells me to dress in my warmest clothes. She holds up my boots, the ones I had spent so long cleaning, and says, "Carry these and don't put them on until you get outside."

It is clear that she has done this before. We creep past Bayles, who is asleep on the chair outside the door. Unlike the other Prefects, she always sleeps. We know the pattern of her snores, loud, thick ones as she drops off to sleep, followed by snuffling when she enters deep sleep.

She is snuffling now. Her head hangs awkwardly to one side and her arms are folded on her lap. In her sleep, and without her eyeglasses, she looks so defenseless. We slip past her as fast as we can, checking only to make sure she is properly asleep.

Once outside, we join Carrow, Ryan, and Pike, who are waiting, pressed against the wall of the Bath House. A surge of excitement and terror crackles through us all. We race along, keeping to the blocks of shadow as we dart one by one across the corner of the Quadrangle and then out under the arch. In the moonlight the words SAINT HILDA'S COLLEGE FOR WOMEN throw their own set of etched shadows upon the stone.

For a single second, before I duck under the arch, I glance back. I thought I saw a light, the flaring of a candle flame on a wall and a figure at one of the College windows, in the wing where the Committee Members are housed. There is a momentary silhouette of a head and shoulders. The Committee Chair, the woman with the yellow glass eye covering? But it is so brief, just the time it takes to snuff a candle. I say nothing and set it to the back of my mind. If we had been seen scuttling like mice across the Quadrangle, the alarm would have been raised by now.

The sky is clear and sparkles with icy stars. Laing leads the way, swerving in and out among the trees. At intervals she stops and looks back to make sure we are keeping up. She moves so fast, so sure-footed. It would be easy to fall behind if we were not all trained to keep up this pace. Nevertheless, for her, a tall, slim figure moving swiftly across the terrain, it seems to be less effortful than for the rest of us.

It is a far longer trail than I had expected. Soon we leave the edge of the forest and start over the ridge and down into the valley. This is not unknown territory, but walking out here at night is making everything sharp and new again. It takes a good twenty minutes for us to reach the river that flows near Bareneed Farm, and I realize that I am shivering although I have on as many layers of wool as I own.

The river is no longer frozen, and the sound of the water loosened from the ice is soothing. Soon Laing veers away from its course, although we are still moving along the bottom of the valley toward a more northerly ridge, one of a series of ridges that separate us from the ocean. We start up the ridge and as we near the top of it, I look down into the valley and the river below. Bareneed Farm is to the west and I can just make out the fences surrounding the outer pastures. We stamp and our breath plumes upon the glittering air, like so many wild horses out for a midnight gallop.

"Get on," urges Laing. "We've hardly got any time left."

And then she vanishes.

I walk a few more paces along the top of the ridge into a stand of pines, then out again the other side, followed by the others.

"Carrow, where has she gone? You will have to lead now."

Carrow's pale face floats in the darkness. She looks plain scared now, no longer excited.

"I have to look again. I only came once before and it is so hard to find. It just looks like an ordinary patch of ground." When she says that, I feel a stab of jealousy, a stab to the heart that leaves me shocked at the force of it.

"You've been here before?" Ryan's voice is squeaky with incredulity and, like me, jealousy. She turns to Pike. "She's done this before," she says again. Pike giggles with pure nerves.

Then we hear Laing's impatient voice as if from below our very own feet. Like a rabbit, her head pokes out from an opening, some kind of slit in the earth that lies in the shadow of the pines. A roof of earth and grass overhangs the opening—we are all practically standing on it and we had never noticed it.

"Get inside. Hurry up." Her head disappears again.

The opening is so narrow that we can pass through only one at a time: first Carrow, then Ryan, followed by Pike. I am the last one inside.

It is the oddest place I have ever seen. A sloping walkway leads into a tunnel that is made of some stuff such as I cannot name: a kind of gray stone lacking in fissures and smoother than almost any rock surface.

It is airless down here with little or no light to speak of. I resist the urge to run back to the opening in order to take great gasps of the clean air and get out from under this roof, so low that it almost touches our heads. It is not a space made for women of our height. The others mill about in front of me until Laing commands us sharply to follow her down the walkway. Now that my eyes have adjusted somewhat, she is standing in front of what looks to be a big metal door at the end of the narrow stone slope.

Again, it is not any kind of door I recognize. It is very wide, more than three or four times the width of a normal door, and its metal surface is lined with a series of narrow, perfectly regular ridges and troughs. At first I cannot see any handle or hinges, but Laing fits both her hands into what I then see are two cunningly placed, hidden slots. Instead of pushing, she pulls. To our amazement, the door does not open inward or outward, but begins to roll upward, producing a harsh sound of metal grating on metal. Although Laing gives it another shove, it seems to gather something of its own momentum. As it rises, it folds and flattens itself along its ridges before coming to rest on metal struts suspended on the ceiling of another dark space beyond. We stare at it, quite speechless.

"If anyone else has ever found this," declares Laing, "they just never managed to figure out how to open the door."

"How did you find it?" Laing knows that I'm challenging her. I can't help it.

"I was out on an errand one day and I took what I thought was going to be a shortcut. The ground was wet, and suddenly I just fell through the earth." Laing eyes me for a second, as if deciding whether or not to say something that will squash me, but she seems to decide that I'm not worth the effort. She fumbles for something in her pocket.

"What are we to do for light?" My voice sounds both flattened and hollow, as if the damp, dead surface around us were drawing in the sound and absorbing it forever, our voices trapped in the stone, if stone it be.

She looks at me, triumphant as she produces a tinderbox and a stub of a candle, both obviously stolen from the Housekeepers since we are not allowed such things without permission. Weak light trembles on the walls of the space that has been revealed by the door, illuminating more of the flat gray stone, divided into blocks like overlarge bricks. The others have become skittish, giggling and whispering, although all I want to do is get out of this barren place that was clearly made in the Time Before.

"Why are you whispering?" I ask. "Who would hear us under the earth like this? We could scream if we wanted and not a soul would hear. We could die here and no one would ever find us."

They take no notice of me. There is too much to look at. The chamber is not as empty as we first thought. In fact, as our eyes and nerves adjust, I see that it is full of objects. There are all manner of flasks and bottles and other kinds of containers pushed into one corner, and to one side are piles of boxes made out of hard brown paper. There are large colored words printed upon them: SUNLIGHT and DOVE. Do the boxes contain these things? A box of sunlight? Of doves? They do not even look to be all that strong, although a few of them are made of wooden slats.

Laing has set her candle down upon the floor and then she commands us to sit. "In a circle," she says. This we do. The floor is both clammy and very hard, another of the unyielding surfaces the Old People fashioned for themselves.

"We don't have much time," she says, still whispering. She takes out a timepiece, another thing she must have stolen, and looks at it and frowns. Then she sets about dragging one of the brown boxes over to our circle. Although it causes her no real difficulty, it seems to be of some weight.

We begin to look around and our eyes are now everywhere, slowly taking in the objects ranged about this square cavern of dead air. Apart from the stacks of hard paper boxes, there are a number of tools hanging on a rack on one of the walls. These include saws, hammers, a couple of chisels, and several other tools I am not familiar with. There is a workbench too, with edges and surfaces so even that, again, it is impossible to imagine the touch of the human hand in its fashioning. The Time Before must have been a time of such smoothness, a time when everything was exact. The Old People must have had the most unerring eye, the steadiest of hands to make everything so perfect, so regular.

My eye wanders, eventually settling on two more contraptions, each with two wheels in direct alignment with each other and held together by metal spars and a central inverted triangle of metal, upon which is a tiny, odd-shaped leather saddle. At one end are a pair of curved metal pipes that look as though they are to be held in some way, and at the apex of the inverted triangle is another mechanism flanked on either side by a small block of something solid that surely must provide some kind of propelling force along cogs and a chain that connects to the wheels. Wheels! How Smith would love to see these objects. I hear her voice, the laughter hidden in her strange question: *Do you think a woman invented the wheel?*

The two machines lean against the wall, and there are many other strange objects stacked or scattered about. A fine layer of dust silts every object and, for a moment, I am consumed with a desire to rub it all away, to drag all of it out into the daylight and gaze for hours upon the hard forms of these things from the Time Before.

"Hurry up!" Laing's eyes shine with almost animal urgency. Her hands flutter above the box she has dragged into the center of our circle. "Look. Look at these!"

She unfolds the flaps of hard brown paper that form the opening of the box and then proceeds to unload more paper. As I catch my breath, my first thought is that here, at last, I am looking at some pages, but they are not the kind of pages I have ever seen. The papers are all bound together, not the separate sheets the Librarian allows me. As if I were drowning, that is the last I remember of normal thought because of the welter and profusion of images.

Images are forbidden to us. The only images we have ever been allowed to see, and then only briefly, were those of the enemy. I do not remember them all that well, just some thick black lines on paper that showed creatures with hairy, heavy bodies given to sweating, with thickened limbs, coarse features, empty eyes, and slack mouths, as if they have trouble breathing through their noses. They are tall but we are as tall. We are also stronger, lighter, faster, and much more skilled. When the images were passed among us, they filled us with contempt and a kind of physical loathing, as though we could smell the grease on their skin, the odor of their sweat.

But these are not images of the enemy. These are images of women. At least I think they are women. There are pages and pages of them. On some of the pages, trails and columns of words swarm around the images like ants. The paper is smoothly glossed to high perfection.

"These women must be the women of the Old People, the Time Before," I say. The sound of my own voice takes me by surprise. A silence has fallen as we gaze, stupefied by what we have found.

"They must have been women from another realm," murmurs Pike.

"The colors and the raiment . . ." Ryan strokes one of the pages, so dazzled that her hand shakes.

Laing, who has solemnly handed each of us one of these page-objects, is radiant with the happiness of sharing what she has found.

"They are the most beautiful things you will have

ever seen. Look," she breathes and holds up her pages for us all to see. "They must have had a different way of walking. Look at the things on their feet."

Each clutching our own set of pages, we gasp at what is strapped to the feet of the women in the images Laing shows us. Boots are what we could have called them, if not for the most peculiar shape: pointed toes and, most astonishing of all, the elongated heels, so sharp they must have been a kind of weapon, or perhaps a tool. In one image, the woman's hair is whipping about her head, as if she were caught in a gale, and she wears a short coat made of what looks to be leather, except that it is bright green. Underneath the green coat, the woman appears to have on no other garment.

"They must have moved around partly naked," I whisper. And I think of the fish-women under their warm, forgiving sun. This woman seems to be standing alone, on an empty plain under a lowering sky, staring, straining to see something in the distance. Her arms are thrown straight to her sides, as if she were in despair. Indeed, she has big dark rings around her eyes. Our own eyes and minds ache with the profusion of the images, images we cannot take in or understand.

"It took me some time," says Laing. "At first I couldn't take it all in. It takes practice. We will have to teach ourselves to look and to understand it all. But once you start, it gets easy very quickly. Your eye learns how to move more slowly over the image instead of being blinded by the colors and the strangeness."

She says to use our forefingers, thus, running it over the glossy page, to guide us and to slow the almost painful flickering of our eyes. But even so, the images are so *other,* so different from anything we have ever seen, that I begin to feel nausea and the familiar throbbing over my left eye.

By carefully running our fingers over the images, some sense does begin to surface. The women from the Time Before were not made of flesh, but instead some other flawless, gleaming material. Perhaps they glowed in the dark. Their lips are dark red and pink; their eyes are enormous, often with dark rings around them. These look to be painted on, or perhaps the women from the Time Before bruised easily around the delicate skin of their eyes. Some of the women, often only partly clothed, are huddled into corners of great rooms with high, gilded ceilings, or they lie about on beds gazing up at something, their limbs at odd angles, as if their bodies had been dropped there and had broken. Yet others, dressed in long flowing gowns, climb trees. They sit on fantastic, delicate chairs or they lie, naked except for colored underwear, upon beds lined up next to a rectangular pool of water so blue it may not even be water. They wear big, black eyeglasses, which make their faces impossible to understand. They wear polished stones and are draped in fabrics and stuffs that must have been spun from the air or rainbows or petals. I cannot think that wool, or leather, or even linen was used in their finery, but when I can force myself to concentrate, I see some signs of these things. I also see fur—capes, coats, hats. Some of it is green or blue or pink, so they must have had completely different animals from the few we manage to trap and kill. I wonder at how they trapped and killed the blue and green and pink creatures.

There cannot have been any stony pathways or trampling horses or earth to plow. They must have had the power to float above the ground whenever they chose. Who then did the work? None of these women could have done any work, for they are so small, with their shoulders and bones poking through their perfect skin like so many starving birds. So many of them smile! How happy they must have been!

"Look," says Pike. "They had girl-children." She shows us an image of a woman wearing a dark green jacket and a belt studded with metal. The woman has a rifle slung over her shoulder and stands with a naked baby on her hip. The woman looks to be very tall, so perhaps these were their warriors, their Trackers. But then we gasp, for the baby is not a girl-child, but a boy-child. There! Alive! Plump and chuckling on the warrior's hip.

Laing then points out something even more shocking.

"Do you see these?" She flicks through a few pages and then stabs at one of the images. She handles the sets of pages with a familiarity we have not acquired. "Did you think they were women? They're not! They are not women! I know because I have been trying to read some of the words, even though I am not good at reading like Keller is. And I found out that they are the enemy! Or at least they are male. They were not the same then. Look!" She points to one of them who is half-naked. He has a lithe, slender body that is carved with muscles; he also has muscular breasts, and nipples.

In total silence we try to take in the image of the creature. Dark, smooth hair, some kind of jacket flung over a shoulder. He looks as though he is sulking. And it is obvious what lies beneath his blue pants. I think of what we laugh at, the stallions and the bulls, the rams, their balls banging about on their hindquarters, purple-black sheaths dangling between their legs. I look doubtfully again at the image.

"They looked like this," says Laing, with her growing authority. "They had this soft, pretty hair and smooth skin and these tight garments on." She gazes and says dreamily, "I suppose they just weren't dangerous then."

We cannot take our eyes off the half-naked boy-male-enemy-being.

"I wonder what they smelled like," says Ryan, at last. Her question, quavering in the semidarkness, breaks our long silence. Our shadows loom and flap on the walls of the square cave and then we are all frightened again, fear crackling through us at what we have opened up.

"How many times have you been here?" My voice is hoarse with fear. "Who else knows about this place?"

Laing holds her candle aloft. It has burned down to the wick and there is only a pool of melted wax and the wick to keep the flame going for a few more minutes.

I look at Carrow's face and she looks back at me, triumphant. "Only me," she says. "Laing has brought only me—"

"We are to make a pact," Laing interrupts her. "No one is to tell. Each time we come here, we come together. No one is to come alone except me, because I found it and I worked out how to open the door. We shall come here and look at the images and objects whenever we can and I shall also show you some of the other things that are to be found in here." She sets the candle down and rummages in one of the boxes, pulling out yet more of the bound-together pages. Although time is running out, Laing is not finished.

She plucks at some object that seems to be fastened to the front page, trying to release it.

"They put gifts here," she says. "They're stuck on to the pages, usually the first page. They were called special offers." She frowns and hesitates. "Or offerings. I forget now. Anyway, watch this." She turns her back and fumbles for a minute or two, hunching over so that we cannot see what she is doing. Then she whips around and her slender shadow whirls with her across the walls of the chamber. Her hands are spread and upon her fingernails are the talons, the very same as the one she displayed to me that day in the tack room.

"My name is Brandi," she proclaims. And for an instant I see it again, the shock of it once more, the letters dripping on the wet windowpane of the tack room.

Laing continues, intoning as if it is the beginning of some kind of ceremony, "That is the name of the most beautiful woman among all the images. Brandi has her fingernails like this and I found these stuck on the front of the page. They were in a little bag made of the most peculiar stuff, like paper that you could see through, and it was very easy to remove them from the page. See? I worked out what you do—you glue them on. Look, Keller, this was what I showed you in the tack room the other day."

Her open mouth is red and wet in the candlelight.

For a few seconds she remains fixed in her position, clawed hands still held up in the frozen motion of one about to grasp a living thing. "If we look hard, we will find more special offerings," she says, her voice shaking with excitement. "It's our secret. Our secret." And she holds one talon up to her lips.

"Shhh," she says. "No one."

CHAPTER FIVE

LAING WAS wrong.

The Committee Members have not left us. As they walk among us, their long furs sway and glint in the sun that has blossomed in a clear, cold sky. What do they do? Why are they here instead of at Johns, the place from which they rule Foundland? Their leader, the one with the screen of yellow glass strapped over her eyes, is the Chair, the most powerful woman in the land, and we watch her as much as we dare.

They wear their hair scraped tight to their skulls and their eyes are keen. So far, although we cannot be certain, they do not seem to be carrying Seed. No impregnations have commenced. Still, no one knows why they have come. It is as if they are sniffing the air, trying to detect some kind of change.

The Members continue to spend many hours in the Library, locking down all the doors. For the past few days I have not been allowed pages to read in the evenings, and have to make do with chess and the humiliation of several defeats at the hands of Laing. Surely they will soon find what they are searching for.

Except on the mountains and high ground, the snow melts and reveals sour yellow grass and black clods of earth that are so unyielding as to make one wonder if it can ever again produce a crop or new grass for the livestock. The rare, easy weather arrives and disappears without warning, just the same way happiness can, descending, then dissolving, then gone.

LAING AND CARROW have told the rest of the Patrol that they are "best friends," and they try to sit together at mealtimes or stand next to each other in the Bath House. They play incessant games of chess and find excuses to touch each other's arms and hands, all the while exchanging a language of looks that seems to mean all kinds of things to them and that excludes anyone else. The rest of us watch this closely and already I think Ryan and Pike are trying to imitate them, going off into corners for no real reason and erupting into bouts of sniggering that will attract the attention of the Prefects soon. The whole Patrol will be punished.

I was almost tempted to say something to my Confidante about it. We each have a Confidante, and I suppose in some way *they* are intended to be our best friends. Except somehow they just aren't. We are supposed to tell them all the thoughts we need to share, the thoughts that would be inappropriate to share with anyone else. Our secrets, I think you could call them. And then, for our own good, the Confidante must share them with the Headmistress.

My Confidante's name is Gosse. She came unexpectedly a few days ago and pulled me out of the early ride. Confidantes tend to do that, just pitch up because they have the right to interrupt anything if they want. When Gosse isn't being my Confidante she works at the salmon pools, and so she often smells of fish meal. She was once a Tracker too, but an injured leg, one that causes her to limp, meant that she had to be reassigned. I don't think she has ever gotten over the humiliation of having to work at the salmon pools, but she accepts her duty, or at least seems to.

She is a nervous sort of person and has worked hard at trying to be the one to whom I tell my worries and my innermost thoughts, but the very fact that she works so hard at it means that all we have ever established is a kind of politeness. Really, it is just an act. She dares not admit to the Headmistress how little I tell her because it would mean failure on her part, and I quite like it that way.

She has a habit of furrowing her brow and pinching the top of her nose with her thumb and forefinger whenever I start telling her anything, then whenever I pause, looking at me very intently, which is not the way to get an easy conversation going. It also startles me and makes me think that I have said something of great importance, which in turn makes me even more guarded.

And now I do have something to hide.

She took me into the kitchens and we sat by the fire. They often sit us down in front of a roaring fire. Perhaps the warmth and the sleepiness it brings on helps to unlock our tongues.

After we had settled ourselves she said, "You look so healthy and you are doing so well on the shooting range."

"I wish I were as good at archery," I said. If I hadn't been so worried about keeping my mouth shut, it would have been quite pleasant sitting there stretched out in front of the fire with tea, listening to the House-keepers banging about in the laundry. We had the kitchen more or less to ourselves. "And I'm getting worse at chess, not better."

This seemed to provide her with some kind of opportunity, because she said quickly, "You still read a great deal? Why do you like it so much?"

I hated her asking this because whatever the answer, more would be revealed than I wanted.

"I just do," I answered sullenly. "It's different from everything else that we do. I can't explain why."

My insolence seemed to work and she was anxious to diffuse my mood. "Is there anything that you are unhappy about?" It was almost unendurable to be courted in this manner. The firelight glowed on our faces and outside a raw wind keened, bringing with it a thin, vicious sleet that would turn into snow again by nightfall.

After a while, I grew tired of my own defensiveness. There was so much that I wanted to know.

"Why are the Committee Members here?" I said. "Have they come to assess us for impregnation? We are all worried. We know what impregnation means. We know how they do it. The Prefects and the Housekeepers tell us more than you think." *We've seen the stallions straddling the screaming mares, the bulls lumbering and maddened with lust,* I wanted to say, partly to mock her. *We all know what they do.*

"We know we're supposed to be grateful that we will never have to endure the daily rape that is the lot of the women beyond." With my foot, I pushed at a log that had slipped, pretending to concentrate on that instead of my real worries. "We'll never be Breeders, so why are they here?"

Gosse became very still. "Well, I admit it is rare for a Tracker to be impregnated, but you don't know if you are a Breeder or not. If we are fertile, then it is our duty to submit to impregnation. The other Novices and the Apprentices have to submit, don't they? Anyway, it happens so seldom that I don't think there is any cause for concern right now. I think they are just here to take a look," she said cautiously. "They do that every now and then. Make the trip from Johns to see the outlying areas in order to survey the domain. And we have been so successful they have come to see for themselves."

One of the Housekeepers came in with baskets of bread, which she put down on the table. Gosse fell silent. She waited until the Housekeeper was well out of earshot before saying in a low voice, "They think there is a rich find somewhere near here. They say there is a whole trove of found objects from the Time Before. If they can locate it, it will be a very important find. There has been talk that they have come to search for it themselves."

I stared straight ahead and said in a voice that was so cold and calm it surprised even me: "What would be in this find?" My heart was knocking at my ribs.

"That I don't know." Having done too much talking, Gosse reverted to being anxious, searching instead for a question to ask me. She has great faith that a single question will crack me open and reveal all. And this time, I do keep talking.

"The thing is, I wish I knew how things worked. There is so much that goes unanswered. It's not exactly that there are lots of secrets, but things get passed over or they are just half-said, and we're not encouraged to ask. We have to keep so busy. We have to be so good at the things we are being trained for. Sometimes I just want to . . ." What I wanted to say sounded ridiculous: "sit still." A brief image of the fish-women lazing on their rocks flickered in my mind. I tried again. "I like to sit and read," I said. It sounded so feeble, but because that was what she had wanted to talk about at the beginning, I thought it would please her. Reading is a source of concern to her, promoting, as she and the Librarian have both mentioned, "inwardness."

She leaned forward and studied my expression in that unnerving way of hers. I had to find a better distraction.

I sighed. "And I get so tired. Especially when I am menstruating." At last Gosse's face cleared. I must have said something that she had been expecting or hoping to hear.

"Oh yes, that can happen. That is normal, you know, to feel tired and sad at that time. It is of no significance, the sadness does not mean anything at all. It is just a mix of fluids in your system and nothing more. You must ignore it and carry on, know that it passes, like so many things." She paused. "Did you tell anyone else that you feel tired and sad at that time of the month?"

"No. I wasn't sure if it was appropriate or not."

"You told me," she said and smiled. "And that was the right person to tell. You don't need to tell anyone else now, do you? I am your Confidante and that is what I am here for." She hesitated and then decided to press her advantage. "It is divisive, you know, to talk here and to talk there, whisper, whisper. We must hold together and hold our tongues. Gossip is for weaker women. Just as tears are useless, so is idle chatter. Weeping achieves nothing and never has. That, and whisper, whisper . . ." She made a quacking motion with her hand. "Silly, empty talk."

She might as well have been describing Laing and Carrow or Ryan and Pike. Whisper and giggle, that is the definition, it seems, of best friends.

But I said nothing more, as if there were some other loyalty pulling me harder in their direction than in the vision that Gosse had offered me, that of fierce, silent Foundlanders hauling away at life together.

IT IS as if Gosse, like the others in authority, refuses to hand me the piece I need to complete the picture I want to make. All I have are such tiny fragments with which to piece together the world around me and to try to solve the puzzle that in some way tempts us all: the riddle of the Time Before, and perhaps, the riddle of the time to come, if there is a time to come. The Old People must have thought they had a limitless future; I think that is just the way of our minds. But the Old People are gone now. The pieces of their lives are lost and scattered in the toxic rods of fire that fell on the earth.

After the hellfire died away, there must have been a vast silence, a kind of long, strange peace. Did the towers of smoke sink back to the earth? Leaving what? A huge quiet sky of purple and gold? An enormous empty beginning? Did the scabbed birds that survived cry out, and then rise upon new and unfamiliar plumage into these noiseless skies? Did the disfigured and warped animals that lived roam free, released unto themselves and their new, terrible ways? Did the lush, deviant leaves unfurl, green and poisoned, into whatever warmth there may have been?

What can I know? What was left? Perhaps an unseen and pulsating world left to its own devices, untouched by our hand. We Foundlanders scrape away at the soil we have left but I think we barely manage. Perhaps we are not as successful as we tell ourselves. I know this is blasphemy but deep in my heart, I have started to see, or at least sense, that things are not as all the authorities will have us believe. Is this why we are so frightened? What lies behind all the rules that govern us? I obey them, and yet these days they chafe me so.

I need to be alone in order to think, but the only way I can do that is to ask permission to go on a walkabout. On a walkabout we are allowed to roam the territory as we desire so that we can practice our survival skills. We are permitted two walkabouts a year. Of course, we are not really either free or alone—we are tracked all the way—but when I have been on walkabouts, I felt as though my burdens were lighter. I didn't tell anyone, of course.

I resolve to request permission for a walkabout, but in the meantime I must find some small comfort in the pages from the Library. At last I have been allowed back in to get hold of some pages, and I have one small special thing that I came across a day or two ago. In among the pages was a whole story. At least it seemed like a whole story, the first that I have ever found in the torn pages. It is about a young woman called Pandora, who lived with a man called Epimetheus in an exquisite garden where there was no toil, no fear, no pain. How slowly the hours must have passed for her, since her life seemed to be one of warm, indolent nothingness.

In this story there was something that suggested that life in this abundant garden, where nothing ever happened, was the perfect life. When at last something happens, there is foreboding; it is all about to be ruined.

A weary, travel-stained being called Mercury arrives in the garden. He is a magical being called a god. He leaves a box tied with a golden cord in the safekeeping of Pandora and Epimetheus, but for no good reason tells them that they must not look inside the box. Pandora and Epimetheus quarrel because Pandora is consumed by the desire to look into the box and, for some inexplicable reason, Epimetheus is not curious. He leaves her alone and goes back into the garden of delight; she creeps over to the box and begins to untie the complicated knot of golden thread that fastens it. She is sure, as she works at the knot, that she can hear whispers from within the box, whispers that beckon and entice her to work even more quickly to undo the knot. The voices beseech her to free them from their prison.

At last the golden cord falls to the floor and she lifts the lid. But before she can do anything, clouds of ugly brown insects fly from the box. They begin to sting mercilessly and bite, and for the first time, both Pandora and Epimetheus experience pain and terror. Pandora has, in her disobedient actions, unleashed all suffering upon the world.

In desperation she attempts to shut the lid on the box, but there is one final voice entreating her to open the lid just once more, a voice that tells her, "I will heal your wounds. I will ease your pain." With so little left to lose, Pandora opens the box once again, and there emerges a beautiful white-winged creature that alights upon their wounds and touches them with a feathered wing tip, relieving them of their pain.

"Who are you?" asks Pandora, and the creature answers: "I am Hope."

In that airless cavern full of strangeness, have we opened some kind of box of evils? Are we, the disobedient members of the Patrol, Pandoras all? But I do know this: I know I shall go back again to that hidden chamber. I won't be able to stop myself.

CHAPTER SIX

THE COMMITTEE MEMBERS seem to be trying to find ways to kill time. They ride a great deal, and they are all skilled. They ride with whips and spurs in order to bend the animals more immediately to their will.

The other day, the Chair, who wears the yellow glass mask over her eyes, did something quite extraordinary.

Most of us were mucking out the stables and doing other chores when she appeared. Hung over her left arm was a very small, dainty saddle. She stood in the yard and watched us for a short time, then summoned Pike and ordered her to catch the young gray mare in the near paddock.

While she was issuing her orders I examined the saddle upon her arm, the shape of which I have never seen before because there was only one stirrup and a very high, hooked pommel. The Chair turned and handed me the saddle. It was so light, and I could feel the buttery softness of the leather. Then the Chair disappeared into the tack room.

To our astonishment she reappeared without her furs, wearing such a costume! She had on a tight jacket with many tiny buttons at the sleeves, and a skirt of deep red that fell to the ground. Where would she obtain such a thing? None of us has ever worn a skirt, although I have heard that in Johns some women do go about in them. How could we do our work, get through our day in such a garment?

After that, she did something even more astonishing. She removed the yellow eye mask and donned the strangest of hats. It was straight and tall and black. Suspended from the brim was a veil of dark netting that covered her face, so you could barely make out her fine, sharp features.

Well aware now that all our eyes were upon her, she mounted. But instead of sitting astride, she sat on the odd-shaped saddle *sideways*! Her legs were concealed by the skirt, and her offside leg was hooked over the pommel while her near leg and foot found a proper place in the lone stirrup. She sat erect and very tall, her torso like a stamen rising up out of the billowing skirt.

We ceased our sluicing and shoveling and craned our necks to watch as she moved the mare forward. Unable to contain ourselves, we dropped our shovels and brushes and followed her out to the arena, and there we formed an audience. Amos saw us go, her whole body taut with this ridiculous display that was beyond her power to prevent. No word was spoken, but it was clear that the leader required some kind of witness to her skill.

She proceeded to put the horse through every pace, even at one point jumping over some logs that were lying on the ground. We gasped. The grace of it was undeniable, but why ride in that manner? What could be achieved by it and how did she come to learn it? It was as if she were out to flout every Pitfall there is and a few more besides.

After she had dismounted and handed the mare back to Pike, she lifted the veil. "Thank you," she said. "I feel so good today! I feel full of life!"

I managed to catch a glimpse of her face before she replaced the yellow glass eye mask. Her mouth was parted and she was panting slightly. Her moist skin was flushed pink, and for a second I saw how her eyes glittered with a kind of crazed happiness before she covered them once again with the mask.

Her name is Ms. Windsor. The Housekeepers tell us that in Johns the women call themselves "Ms." *Mzz* is how you say it. "Yes, mzz," we say, on the rare occasion we have to speak to the Committee Members. And there is one more thing about Ms. Windsor.

When she is not spreading a low level of fear or shocking us with her riding antics, she too spends a great deal of time in the Library. I have seen her name in the Ledger and that is how I know.

Her fantastic moment caused in us a kind of frivolity, but sideways-riding or not, the Committee Members frighten us with their constant silence and cold observation, their mysterious to-ings and fro-ings as they sweep through the Quadrangle in their furs with their hair scraped to their skulls in tight coils.

At supper our Patrol scuffles in the line to get our food.

"What is it called, that way of riding?" Laing says to Carrow. They are sitting together, heads bent in toward each other. "It was just so beautiful." She sounds wistful. "If we were allowed to talk to the Committee Members, then I would ask her if she could teach me." Now that we have had a chance to see her close up, we are all spellbound by Ms. Windsor, despite our fear of her. Laing is particularly fascinated. "Did you see her hands?" she breathes. "She has perfect pink fingernails. No dirt."

Carrow notices me eavesdropping and, drawing herself up over Laing's head, regards me coldly. It is to tell me to go away, that this is theirs alone and I am not wanted. I return her gaze, but only for a moment or two because I am suddenly filled with a terrible misery. I feel my shoulders sag, as if something I wanted is to be barred from reach forever.

Carrow drops her head once again into the intimate little circle of two, and they resume their forbidden whispering until one of the Prefects comes and tells them to shut up.

The Prefects seem nervous tonight. At every excuse they snap and snarl. The Housekeepers enter and bang about, clearing away the dirty dishes. This time at night, after a day of chores, they are always bad-tempered as they finish up with their duties.

When the Headmistress comes into the Refectory flanked by the Committee Members, the Housekeepers are as surprised as we are, although the Prefects seem to have anticipated it and have already lined up along one wall. A hush falls over the whole Refectory. Then a mug, teetering on the top of a pile of dirty dishes, falls and smashes to the floor, and the noise it makes is as if a loud and terrible sin has been committed. The red-faced Housekeeper gathers it up under the shocked gaze of all but the Headmistress, who is unperturbed as usual. She holds herself erect in her usual manner with her still hands and her still body. She always makes as few unnecessary movements as possible, as though she has learned over a long lifetime what is and what is not a worthwhile use of her energies.

The Headmistress is the oldest person I have ever

seen, though she is far from feeble. Her eyes hold all her experience. You can see all her long life in them, yet the story of it is still withheld. Her hair has not turned fully gray; there are strands of gold in it. It is dry and coarse now, cut short but still thick. Perhaps she was once beautiful like Laing.

She never raises her voice and yet it is always audible from wherever you may be standing. As she speaks now, it is in the same even tone as always.

"You are to stop whatever you are doing," she says. "Line up and enter the Hall. As of this moment you are all under a vow of silence. There will be no word spoken for a full seven days. It is forbidden to make any unnecessary sound."

The silence in the room is complete. It seems we are afraid now even to allow the air to pass from our lungs or to draw it in again. We all know what her words mean. There is to be a Silent Beating, tonight, within the hour.

We file out, and the sounds we make—the movement of the cloth upon our bodies, our footsteps, the sound of our breathing—seem jarring now, and loud and sinful. The Housekeepers, still frozen in place holding their piles of dirty crockery, wait until we have left to continue cleaning up, so that if they make a sound it shall have no other witness.

In less than fifteen minutes the girl-children have been marshaled into place. I try not to look at their wide-eyed bewilderment. For many of them, this will be the first time they have witnessed a Silent Beating. What will they remember after it is over? They themselves will be whipped if they make so much as a peep during or after the ceremony.

The Committee Members file onto the stage and take their places on the folding metal chairs from the Time Before. The chairs are brought out on special occasions. We assemble on the bare floor in front of the stage. The Housekeepers and Prefects have come in now, as well as all the other Patrols, the workers, and the few Trackers who are not out on border duties.

I would like to turn and stare at the Trackers. They are infrequent visitors, living as they do out in the wilderness most of the time. They return on occasion, in pairs or small groups, always arriving unannounced, leading their tired horses into the stable yard. They are exhausted themselves, and quite filthy after weeks of camping in all weathers. They stay in the barracks with the Instructors, not with us, and they do not stay long. I have seen dried blood on their clothing once or twice, and covertly I try to check for any further signs of capture or struggle. Tonight, though, I do not dare move my head to look at them.

There is a pause until the Headmistress takes up her position on the stage in front of the Prefects, from whom she will choose two to administer the beating. The Prefects stare straight ahead, their faces deathly pale. But then the Headmistress does something that I do not remember being part of normal procedure. Then again, it is so long since we last witnessed a Silent Beating. When Ms. Windsor enters, the Headmistress crosses the stage. With a tiny gesture, she indicates that Ms. Windsor, not the Headmistress, is to step up and choose the two Prefects who will administer the beating. The two women pass each other on the stage and, though I cannot be certain, there is something peculiar about the way the Headmistress looks at Ms. Windsor, as though beseeching her, pleading, even. But Ms. Windsor appears not to notice. She surveys the Prefects. Despite their enjoyment of doling out petty punishment, I cannot think that any one of them wants to be chosen. I study their faces: Ross, Pearson, Gower . . . and it is only then, with a sick flutter of realization, that I see one of them is not here! Who is missing? The person who is not present is the person to be punished. Now I know why the Prefects were so jumpy, so nasty tonight at supper.

Bayles! Where is Bayles?

As my cheeks turn hot, I hang my head so that no one will notice. No one except the Headmistress and whoever caught the miscreant is ever allowed to know the reason for a beating. And it remains secret forever.

But this time I think I know why Bayles is to be punished. Someone saw us leave the Dormitory that night while Bayles was on duty. This must be her punishment for letting us escape—and we are next! After the beating, they will come and tell us that we are to mount the stage.

My mouth is parched and there is a kind of rushing sound in my ears. Ms. Windsor takes the whips from the basket and hands them to Ross and one of the newer Prefects called Underwood.

They step forward as Bayles is led in dressed in a white shift, underneath which she is naked. Her breasts loll and roll beneath the fabric, and her muscled, hairy legs and large feet stick out from the bottom. Patches of her sweat have already spread from her armpits and she, like me, is trembling. She stumbles as she crosses the stage and looks ever so briefly at us, the assembled company, and her expression is apologetic—and sad.

That is when I see the truth of it. Bayles is not a bully or tyrant. She is instead something that now seems worse: a terrible pleaser, a devoted and submissive servant.

Ross takes the scold's bridle and places it over Bayles's head, strapping it as if she were indeed bridling a horse. She ducks around the front and checks to make sure the iron straps are fitted correctly and that the iron prong is firmly clamped on to Bayles's tongue. She does this in a matter-of-fact way, exactly as one would check that the bit in a horse's mouth was sitting correctly. Bayles's eyes bulge from behind the metal grid and her mouth gapes like a hooked fish, but she makes no sound, not even a grunt, as they begin with the whips. She makes no sound when she falls and is made to get up. She makes no sound when the first blush of pink begins to spread upon the white cloth.

Not a sound do we make, not even the girl-children who know they must watch, watch and learn.

AS THE WEEK wears on, a huge warm sun appears. In silence, the Housekeepers give out linen clothing that liberates our bodies from the hated woolen garments but not from our shroud of silence.

Bayles, swollen and inching around with small, painful steps, is made to rejoin us. She is somehow diminished and we do not look at her as she passes by. After the Silent Beating, we do not dare go to the hidden chamber. Laing, sensing our anxiety, is angry—so angry that, once again, she does the unthinkable and dares to speak during the vow of silence.

"I want to go back," she says to me one day as we are saddling up. Her face is buried in the side of her horse, but I can hear her. "It's the best thing we'll ever get to do."

"I think they know. I think they saw us go. That must be why Bayles got punished." My voice is croaky from lack of use, and I feel almost dizzy with disobedience. But I am pleased because, in this violation of the rules, Laing has chosen to do it with me. She picked me. I pluck up the courage for one more sentence.

"They're waiting for us to go again so that they will have proof." I don't know what I am saying. I just know that I am scared.

Laing finishes saddling her horse and mounts up, one single movement, as though she were weightless. She looks down at me. "It's no fun doing things alone," she says. "Please, let's go there. Just you and me." She's pleading but she's also worried that none of us will want to go with her to that place, and that we might wriggle away from the hold she has over us, her friends.

Because she cannot speak all that she wishes to say, she cannot persuade us otherwise, but her eyes blaze at us lest we turn away.

AT LAST, after what seems longer than seven days, we gather again in the Hall for the Sing that releases us from our vow of silence. At the signal from the Headmistress, wave upon wave of sounds without words rise and rise as the long, sweet notes form a sinuous song that we know but cannot remember learning. Our voices, aching back to life again, fly into the air in what must be joy and renewal. All I want to do now is get away.

CHAPTER SEVEN

"IT IS NOT allowed."

Amos is mending a saddle. Every now and then, when the needle proves inadequate, she leans over the saddle and pulls at the thread with her stained teeth. When she tells me that my request is to be denied, she does so through her clenched teeth, yanking at the thread and tugging it hard through the leather. Amos never talks to anyone without doing something. However, once she has bitten off the thread and inspected the edges that she has now finished stitching together, she does pause for a moment to study my face. "No one goes on walkabouts when the Committee Members are here."

"But we don't know how long they are going to stay. They could be here forever." I too look as if I am doing something, since I am holding a bucket of water that I filled for no special reason other than to look busy. I put down the bucket because I cannot take any more pretense. "I'm begging you," I say softly. "I need to go. I need to get out and be alone for a while. And I am owed a walkabout. I have taken only one this whole year and I need to see the ocean. Please. Give me five days."

"Why?" Amos picks up another saddle. "Why do you need to be alone? We are a community," she says, "are we not? We are not supposed to *like* being alone, except insofar as it is necessary to develop self-sufficiency. And we are here to support one another, so that we do not ever feel lonely. We are united. That is true, is it not, Keller?"

I stare at her. This is not the kind of thing Amos normally says. And there is something in her tone that I cannot place, as if she were toying with me in some way, as if expecting me to contradict her. I have never been denied permission to go on a walkabout. It is not as though I were truly expecting to be alone, because the Trackers are always with us even if we cannot see them.

I begin to shuffle about, wondering where this talk is leading. What does she want me to say? But she is the one who speaks. Her voice is still the same, a little playful, again as if encouraging some response in me that I am ill-equipped to give. "But then again, you can be in an agony of loneliness and longing even though you are surrounded by living, breathing humans, can you not? And when there is no soul in sight, you can feel a carefree companionship with the empty air and sky. There is solitude and then there is loneliness. It is an interesting distinction, don't you think?"

She gets up and puts the saddle back on its peg, then reaches for her tobacco tin. I feel as though she has peeled away my outer protection, and all my loneliness and confusion is on display. Scared that I might begin to cry, I concentrate on the painted lid of her tobacco tin. It is decorated with sprigs of a plant that I do not recognize. Again my eyes travel over that large word, which is still legible if incomprehensible: *Altoids*. And other faint words, if I squint: *Curiously Strong . . . Spearmint*. Did the Old People have spears?

I wait while she rolls her cigarette, deft as always, and I hope, as she draws in the forbidden pleasure, her resolve will soften. She's taking her time. With her forefinger and thumb, she removes a shred of the tobacco from her tongue. For Amos, it's a strangely delicate gesture. She takes a second pull at her cigarette. She's waiting for me to say something.

"We work together, it is true. But that does not mean that sometimes we . . . I feel the need to be alone. It does not mean I am being disloyal. . . ." This is new ground for me and I am very shaky upon it. But she does not seem to be listening now. Her gaze has been drawn to some other part of the room behind me. She's always looking, always noticing the things that are out of place or the tasks that have been left unfinished, the chores hastily or improperly completed. I follow her gaze and see that she is looking at the very remarkable long hat and veil worn by Ms. Windsor on that most amazing occasion when she rode the mare sitting sideways, her skirt flowing around her.

The hat has been placed on top of a cupboard, still looking strange but robbed of its true effect without the splendor of its wearer. Nevertheless, when I turn back to face Amos I see that her expression has turned to a black scowl. She marches over to the cupboard, takes her whip, and with one crack knocks the hat off. It tumbles to the floor whereupon Amos all but kicks it. Instead she opens the cupboard door and flings it inside, locking it away. Then she turns and considers me again. I must look as desperate as I feel.

"Okay," she says. "You can go. I'll see to it. I will vouch for you."

She makes to leave, but just as she reaches the door she stops.

"You see, Keller, that woman, Ms. Windsor, makes the rules, so I guess that means she can break them too. The thing is, if we break the rules, what then?" Her tone drips with bitter sarcasm. "A folly," she says, in another tight little voice that I immediately understand to be an imitation of Ms. Windsor. "That's what she told me by way of explaining that riding performance of hers the other day." She stops then and rolls another cigarette, lighting it and inhaling deeply. Suddenly she grins.

"This is my best friend," she says, looking at the cigarette, and then she tosses her bald head just as if she were tossing a thick mane of hair. I stare at her. She grins again and gestures with the cigarette before walking out the door, leaving nothing but the smell of her smoke behind her.

I'm sure she was doing a second imitation: Laing!

THE FOLLOWING MORNING, still worried by this strangest of exchanges, I lead out the mare that I have been given for my walkabout. I have planned to cover as much distance as I can at first, but then I want to be free of the mare so that I can go down the cliffs to the ocean.

The wind has dropped and the sun is still quite high, a good couple of hours away from the horizon. The mare is not pleased with me. She flattens her ears and sidles, rolling her eyes and flinging her head up. It's all the more annoying because I am riding bareback so that I don't have to bother about the saddle when I let her go. I know she will turn tail and gallop back as fast as she can—she is hating this, being away from the stables and the other horses. How they hate to be alone and how glad I am to be solitary!

Amos and her peculiar words come back to me once again. Why are Smith and Amos asking me these unanswerable questions about women inventing wheels and breaking rules and being lonely? Are they teasing me? Is it some kind of test?

I wish they would leave me alone. Do they suspect something about our discovery of the hidden chamber? Is that what they are after?

All I want now is to look out over the open glitter of the ocean and the great, heaving swell of it, like the boiling glass that I once saw when the glassblower passed through the outlying lands. I will watch the birds, tethered to their immense freedom, moving up and up through that air and light, and I too will think myself free.

I dismount and throw my pack to the ground. The mare is already trembling with anticipation of release and wheeling in circles as I try to remove the bridle. I yank her to a standstill and the minute the bridle slips over her head, she is off. All I can hear is her drumming hooves for a few moments more. I catch one last glimpse of her streaming up the side of the stony valley down which we have just come, and I think how her heart will thud with fear until she nears home and the safety of the herd.

And yet, after she has gone I feel a little bereft, the absence of her warmth perhaps, or just her living presence. I sling my bow over my shoulder, pick up my traps and my pack, and begin to climb the last ridge. I can already smell the sea, but I am not there yet. I will have to stop when night falls and wait for first light before I can get to my cliff-top lookout, the special ledge where I can sit and dangle my legs and look far out and beyond.

For tonight I find a good sheltering rock. I set the rabbit traps I have brought and collect some kindling to get the fire going. Then I lie flat on my back and stargaze for a while, marking the constellations off one by one until I tire of that and let them just become a vast scatter of silver with no meaning. Perhaps in the orderly Time Before, when there were seasons, everything had more meaning. Apparently, or so Smith says, at one time this land was covered in snow for many, many months and there were enormous tracts of ice that melted away when the rods of fire rained upon the earth. There were many animals and the sea was thick with sea ice. Big white bears that hunted for seals lived on the ice, but they drowned or starved when it melted away.

At least night and day can be relied upon, even for us, the ones who have been left to make atonement for the sins of the Old People. It's just that no one seems to know what those sins were.

I climb into my sleeping papoose and use my pack as a headrest. There are the rustlings of the night creatures, the mice and the voles, perhaps a fox. With any luck, one or two rabbits will end up in the traps I have set. I feel around in my pack to make sure I have my good knife with me because I prefer slitting their throats to breaking their necks. There is something about the sound of disconnecting a fragile pattern of living bone that I cannot bear.

FAR INTO the night, on the rock behind me, something slithers.

I am still half asleep, not sure of what it is I have seen. A glint of something? Something silver and brown slips away and out of sight. It makes no sound. It had scales, more like fish skin than anything, but there was only the tiniest glimpse. It could have been any manner of creature, but my skin tingles. It is as if, for a moment, a rule has been broken. There are no snakes in Foundland and there have never been snakes. We do not use the word *serpent*. The Librarian knew she had done wrong the day she allowed me the pages containing the story of the serpent in the garden. A brief dread churns within, but I am sleepy and the firelight is dying now. Perhaps it was a dream and no such thing slithered past me at all.

The next morning I check the traps and find a single shivering rabbit inside one of them. Trying to ignore the thin whistle it makes in its fear, I dispatch it. Once it has stopped twitching, I remove its head and feet, gut it, flay it, and rinse it off in a stream to cool the meat, then pack it in some salt and wrap it up for later. I want to cook it on the beach tonight, but first I want to get to my cliff-top lookout. I want to sit above the water, looking out far beyond to the parts unknown.

It's easy to find the ledge because it is so distinct, a large, pale slab of stone hanging out over the water like a natural bench. The sound of the ocean is like breathing, the earth breathing through its own heaving water, beneath its own measureless sky. The seabirds rise and drop on the currents of air that move above the currents of water. All is motion, all is meant to be. If I inch forward from the ledge where I am sitting, I will plummet to my death.

The sound of the sea makes me drowsy, but I don't want to go down to the beach just yet. I place a few rocks in a line around me and lie down. If I doze off and roll, the rocks will stop me from falling. The sun is warm on my back and I do, in fact, drift into sleep. When I waken, to my astonishment, it is already dark. Clouds have come in and a sliver of a ghost moon casts a faint sheen on the sea.

Now I need to get out and go down to the little beach, where I can set up camp and cook the rabbit I have in my knapsack. Hunger makes me hurry and I am moving too fast for the incline and the darkness. Suddenly I am falling, tumbling over and over, a blur of not knowing which end is up. By the time I come to a standstill, I have fallen more than halfway down to the sea and there is a sharp pain shooting through my right ankle. I curse loudly and, for a terrible moment, almost give way to tears, more out of frustration than pain. I get up, swallow hard, and keep going.

I go straight down to the edge of the sea, pull off my boot, and cool my ankle in the water. The sea breaks and swells and I keep looking up and out to sea, as though something should be coming toward me. I feel so unsettled, certain that someone or something is watching me. The earlier mist thickens into clammy fog, and the moon has disappeared. I put my boot back on and limp around, gathering driftwood for a fire.

After my meal, I am filled with a nervous, heightened energy, and I know that I am not going to be able to sleep. Despite my sore ankle, I get up and kick sand over the embers of the fire. A walk it will have to be—anything to get through this night.

I decide not to carry my pack, and store my belongings behind a rock. I start up toward the northern end of the shoreline. I cannot shake off this feeling of something untoward, some presence that I cannot name.

After some time, my foot is hurting too much and

I have to stop and rest. I find the mouth of a shallow cave and sit down, trying to rub the pain away. Again, I sense something is not as it should be.

Some way out, and only just visible, is the tiniest point of orange light: two flashes, a pause, a couple more flashes. It takes a few beats to sort my thoughts from my initial shock, but then I am certain.

There is only one thing it could be—the enemy.

It *has* to be the enemy. And it is then I realize that I am unarmed. Like a complete fool, I left my bow and quiver behind a rock way down at the other end of the beach. I can hear Amos already, the scorn curdling her voice. In the dark I feel my cheeks flush with shame. I look out again—two more flashes, then nothing. I wait and try to think clearly.

We do not leave the land, nor do we travel by sea. It is the enemy that come in their crude, leaky seacraft, attempting to invade us and take away what we have built. I try to sort my thoughts. There must be Trackers here too. They know that I am here, and they will be close by. Through my fear, I also feel a tremor of excitement. I look up again and see one more flash. The light is moving toward the nearest cliff, the one that appears to fall straight to the water. The dark drop of the cliff is menacing and I can't see how they could land there. The light flickers twice, then twice again. Is it my imagination, or is there a pattern? If it is a pattern, then to whom are they signaling? Perhaps some of the enemy might already have landed and they are signaling to one another. I stand up. The craft is close enough now for me to hear the slap of the waves upon it and to see that there is a kind of noisy box at the rear, from which comes a faint puttering noise. Eventually the craft is near enough to make out the figure of the enemy, or at least one of the enemy. A man! For the first time! A man whose face is shielded by a shapeless hat and whose body is concealed in a long, flared oilskin coat stands on the deck, holding the lantern that emits the glimpses of light.

I peer out into the fog again. The puttering noise made by the craft has stopped. I strain to see where the boat has gone but it is no longer there. It's just gone—disappeared.

I examine the cliff again and, as my eyes adjust, I see what it really is—not a single mass, but a cliff that is cleaved almost in two, the split so fine that it is imperceptible at first. Into that sliver of space there is the narrowest of passages, just wide enough to allow and then conceal the craft that is slipping between its ramparts. There is no choice but to creep in the shadows of the cliff and slide into the passage, hiding behind whatever cover I can find. The fog rolls in and I am grateful for it. There is a narrow ledge at the base of the cleft as I clamber through, but the rocks are slippery where the sea boils over and more than once I almost slip. But there are handholds and nooks in which it is possible to hide whenever the fog is too thin to rely upon for cover. It takes more time than I would like, but eventually I am through the little passage. Protected by a crevice, I see the craft as it moves away from me through the first and narrowest part of the passage. Farther along, the passage widens into something even more perfect for the landing of an invader. A small cove is tucked into the cliffs, with a beach that shelves to the water.

The craft moves toward the beach and two of the enemy splash ashore. Is there no one here to attack them? I wait, but nothing happens.

I can hear the enemy's voices now, a fascinating pitch to them, as we have been warned. They grunt and growl, we have been told, although that is not quite what I am hearing. The notes of their talk, though very deep, seem remarkably similar to ours, even though I cannot hear actual words.

Finally they pull the boat partway up the little beach and tie it like a horse to an upright rock. There are three men in the raiding party. The one in the long coat begins throwing a few small sacks to the first two. It must be weaponry and supplies, yet the sacks seem to be full of something soft, like grain.

Unarmed and useless, I am nevertheless desperate to get a better look. I creep farther toward the beach, where I can see a group of large boulders that might provide me with a hiding place. In order to get to them, I have to run across a stretch of open sand, and even when I do reach them, I am not certain they give me sufficient cover. Although my curiosity is pushing me to do reckless things, at least I am close enough to see something of their faces.

What faces! So lined and weathered, just like the very cliffs themselves. And they are tall, taller even than I am. With absolute clarity, I can see that they are mutants. The first man in the oilskin has a huge, deviational humpback and his limbs, though muscular, dangle from his warped body like spider's legs. The other one has a face that is almost concave and his eyes bulge horribly. As for the third, he is very tall and lanky with his deformities perhaps hidden beneath his clothes. They all look as though they have been stretched and distorted. When their oilskins part, they seem to be wearing an assortment of leather clothing that is patched and beaten up. And yet in some ways, they seem to behave as we do, walking more or less normally, organizing their supplies and talking in quiet voices.

Once they have arranged a few of their small sacks, they seem to settle, sitting on the sand and passing a bottle of some liquid between them. For a raiding party, they do not seem in the least warlike. The thought occurs to me that they are waiting for more of their kind, that they are the advance party, because that is all they seem to be doing: waiting.

And then they come, materializing out of the shadows. I know the shapes—our own! Four of them! Once more I curse this foggy night. Just as I need to see for myself who they may be and how they are approaching, the fog finds this hidden crack in the shoreline and rolls in over everything. Dimly I see them making their way toward the beached craft and the seated enemy, who have their backs to them. But from what I can see, something is very wrong. They are walking *toward* the men, taking no cover at all. My heart beats so fast and so loud, I am almost certain they can hear it. The Foundlanders are walking into an ambush because they clearly have no idea that the enemy are sitting there, right before them! I will have to shoot first and I reach for my bow—only to remember that I have no weapon. The first encounter with the enemy and I have failed. I am useless. I hear one of the women call out softly. "Tom," she says. "We made it."

The men let out a low cheer.

I slump against the rock. My legs feel weak. It takes me several minutes before I can find the word for what these women are.

Traitors.

We have traitors in our midst. The thought had

never, ever crossed my mind. The fog rolls around me and I am thankful now that I have something to conceal my presence. I sit for I do not know how long. Who are they, these women? Will Trackers soon pour down from the cliffs to capture these traitors? I wait but there is only the fog and the lack of moonlight—just the cover they need for this forbidden meeting. I try to see if I can recognize them, but I am too far away and the fog keeps coming in. For the most part they are obscured and all I can hear is their mingled voices. It is obvious that they think themselves unobserved, either by me or any Trackers. And then the realization creeps upon me: these women *are* Trackers.

I hear the clink of bottles. Are they drinking something? There is quiet laughter, murmured conversation. At some point I smell something I do recognize: cigarette smoke. Through the thickening fog, the glowing tips of their cigarettes are the only things I can see.

I know not how long this meeting goes on. In all my shock and confusion, I cannot measure the passage of time. When I risk another look, the fog is clearing. The women are making to leave. Their backs are to me as they stand up and brush the sand off their pants. A few bottles are scattered around, which they pick up and hand to the men. Then they do something even more extraordinary and gather the supplies that the men have brought ashore! They load them into knapsacks, all the while exchanging their casual laughter and conversation with the men. Outrage replaces my confusion and I want to stand up and yell at them, tell them they deserve the worst punishment we can mete out. And yet . . . there is something else hovering at the edges of my anger. I am fascinated by their happiness, the easy companionship of them all sitting together, talking and laughing, drinking and smoking deep into the night.

A wave of fatigue overwhelms me. Perhaps I will just sleep here for the night, curled in the shelter of the rock that has guarded me. The women are now moving back up their secret cliff path, although one lags behind, standing to one side with the man with the humpback and spider limbs. Too tired now to bother to properly hide myself, I watch. She is small, lithe like a weasel, and eager. She reaches a hand to his face, tilts her own to his, and he stoops down and their lips meet. At that very moment, for one split second, the moon sails forth, turning the whole beach silver-white, and I see her.

And then I know what I already knew but could not believe until I had no choice.

The woman in the man's arms is Amos.

CHAPTER EIGHT

THE AIRLESS CHAMBER feels almost safe.

In a kind of daze I had traveled toward the secret place underground, the place with the dead air and the strange door. This is a place where I can hide forever.

I had forgotten about my ankle in all the confusion and horrible thrill of what has happened, but now it has become painful again. I limped at times back over the ridge, dropping down into the valley too careless, I fear, of whoever might see me. After a brief search, I found the opening to the hidden chamber.

It was easy enough to imitate Laing's actions when I lifted the bizarre metal door. It is true, it requires a kind of knack, and it was noisier than I remembered.

Laing is going to be so angry with me. What if someone has seen me? What if loyal Trackers have seen me come here? What if the traitors have seen me? Either way, I will have given away our secret.

But this is the place I want to be—a dark, buried place where no one can hear you. I want a place where I can weep.

When the tears start to fall, I make no attempt to stop them. Who can hear me? I howl like a wild animal, then subside into sobs that seem hauled up from my very guts.

Is weeping such a sin? Are my headaches, which I have to work so hard to hide, such a weakness? Is fatigue something so terrible it must never be admitted? We are strong, but we are lonely.

There is solitude and then there is loneliness. What was Amos trying to tell me? Maybe she was trying to turn me against our community. I thought she was a loyal Instructor, not this . . . this other thing.

Loneliness. Solitude.

Wild thoughts come to me as a kind of chant: There is guidance and then there is control. There is order and then there is rigidity. There is cooperation and then there is obedience. These thoughts move so rapidly I cannot pin them down, nor do I know where they even come from. I wish they would stop. I fear the pain that will soon start to throb above my left eye, but for some reason it does not come.

I need light. I still have my tinderbox; we are allowed to take one with us on walkabouts for the purpose of lighting fires. The stub of the candle, once lit, seems to throw more shadow than light, but it will have to do. And once I have collected myself, I see almost immediately something that I did not see the first time.

There it is: a flight of steps leading to a door, actually more like the shadow of a door. I get up, my hand outstretched, ready to touch the outline of what I have become convinced is there. My fingertips meet rough wood, as rough as anything we make, and I see that a series of planks is nailed into place. I glance up at the tools hanging on the wall, some that I can name and some that I cannot. I take what I decide is a crowbar. "A crowbar is a crowbar," I mutter, and begin to work at the planks. They are weak with age and come away within a half hour or so to reveal the real door behind them.

It is hardly a surprise yet I feel the first flickers of excitement. This could be my gift to Laing, a kind of penance for breaking her rule and coming here alone. *There is a door,* I will say. *There is more here than we think.*

Will she thank me? She'll just get mad. I should have waited and dazzled her, and Carrow and Ryan and the others, with what I have just done, revealing this plain wooden door. If it were popularity I was after, I guess I would have.

I place my hand cautiously on the doorknob and

turn. It is locked. And before I know it, temper seizes me. The hole I make in the door with the crowbar, and the speed with which I do it, shocks me. I don't know how long I smash and hack at the door, but all I remember is a kind of giddy exhilaration of destruction until, quite suddenly, it ceases. I step back, spent and panting, hanging my head as shame floods in to replace the rage. The splintered wood lies in pieces at my feet and the beautiful smooth doorknob has been dislodged.

There is a room beyond, and another door. Perhaps beyond that there are yet more rooms. All this while we have just been dithering in some outer chamber, oblivious to what we have really discovered. I have stepped over something more than just a threshold, but I could not stop myself. My candle is burning out; I badly need more light. All I see are shapes that I cannot make sense of. I move forward like a blind person, touching, smelling the musty, locked-away odor of the place. What is this place? Everything beneath my fingers is furred with dust, but still, I can feel the smooth surfaces from the Time Before. I think I know what it could be: a dwelling.

I feel my way, unseeing and frightened, wondering if I might fall into some kind of trap or pit from which I would never escape. The candle goes out and the blackness is complete. It is all too much. I have no light left and my heart is empty. My stores of courage are depleted. I must go back home, to work and to training, back to my own people. I no longer know anything and my world has turned upside down.

I back away and get myself out of the dwelling as fast as I can in the total dark. The hasty job of nailing a few planks back over the door is pointless—anyone could see that it has been opened but, in a feeble attempt to make amends for my tantrum, I do it anyway. I collect my knapsack, grapple with the upward-lifting cavern door, and leave. Enough of dark and oppressive holes in the ground.

The night air is cool. There is no wind and the trees beneath the stars are still. A single tremulous call of a loon on the ponds of Bareneed Farm reminds me that soon it will be dawn. I take a few deep breaths. In the east the sky is turning pink. I set off, hoping my ankle will hold up. Not far to go until I am returned to my own, if that is what they are.

I must be careful.

"YOU SEEM DIFFERENT." Laing's voice echoes in the Bath House.

It took me a long dragging day of walking to get back from the hidden place, but my ankle, though tender, is not painful and I no longer need to limp. I hated limping. It reminded me of Gosse. But I am filthy and the idea of getting clean with plenty of hot water and soap is welcome. Most of the Patrol members have left and the Bath House is almost empty.

Laing is in a good mood. She talks loudly, seeming to enjoy the way the sound of her words bounces off the tiles. She has wrapped her wet hair in a towel, twisted in such a fashion that it forms a ludicrous cone-shaped hat on her head. It must be something she has seen in one of the slender sets of pages from the cavern. If one of the Prefects sees it, she will be reprimanded at the very least. It definitely qualifies as a fad.

"How different?" I pour water from my bucket in a warm river over my body. I wish it would last forever. Laing shrugs and then tips her head forward, untwisting the towel and vigorously rubbing her hair dry. Carrow appears from behind one of the partitions, ever jealous of any conversation between Laing and me. She too has the towel-headwrap business upon her head.

"She *means* since your walkabout," Carrow says. She has started to speak for Laing, or at least act as a kind of interpreting, scornful echo. I could hit her.

"Does she?" I snap. "Is that what you mean, Laing?"

Laing looks up from under her mop of hair. "You just seem quieter than usual. Like your mind is not on anything. Are you depressed, sister?"

I glare at her. *Sister*? When did we ever call each other that? She's an idiot. The conversation is taking a turn that is unfamiliar territory to us all. We are not accustomed to asking one another about our feelings; it is discouraged. Talking about your feelings is what your Confidante is for.

Depressed. The word is unfamiliar although I gather it means sad, perhaps even inconsolable. It is one of the phrases that both Laing and Carrow now use, words plucked from the pages Laing so worships and then echoed by her faithful follower. They half understand the words—"Catch you later," they say under their breath, or "a total disaster" and "no way." They like to say that they're "stressed out," but I don't think they even know what they are saying. I don't.

Laing is still looking at me expectantly. Carrow is hovering. I pull up my towel to cover the nakedness that felt normal just seconds ago.

"I'm not . . . that. I just went a long way," I say. I must be careful. "Farther than I thought. It was perhaps a bit too much. I'm still . . . tired."

Laing's eyes glint. She cannot help herself, and in a way neither can I. She knows me better than I think. I know her better than she thinks.

"I went to the secret cavern," I say flatly.

Carrow gasps.

"You promised along with the rest of us that you would not go alone." Laing doesn't sound as mad as I thought she would be. I realize that she knows I have found something more.

"I found a door. Another door." She is so inquisitive that I know she will just have to ask for more. "There is another room beyond that first room," I say. The color rises in her cheeks. "I think there may be more rooms. Perhaps it is a dwelling of some kind, a dwelling from the Time Before." It is a direct challenge to her ownership of the discovery and we both know it. I do not care. I am not her follower, I am not her servant. I will do as I please, as I think fit. If she wants to be my friend, it is to be on this premise. We are to be equals and nothing else.

Laing hesitates. Her expression is thoughtful, then she smiles and claps her hands. She begins a kind of dance, a squirming hip-wriggle around the towel that she has dropped on the floor. "Oh yeah! Oh yeah!"

She reverts to her normal voice. "What was there? Tell me! Tell me! I knew it! What did you find?" Her questions tumble one after the other and she grasps my hands.

"I had no more light left. I couldn't explore it."

"Oh, awesome!" she says, waiting the fraction of a second it takes for her new word to be acknowledged. "Truly awesome! We'll go soon. Very soon."

"We need to go back with more light, and more time." How we are to do this, I have no idea.

As if planning to go this minute, Laing grabs her clothes and begins to dress. "We'll all go," she declares. "The same ones that went last time. All of us."

Now it is my turn to shrug. Laing is not an easy victory. I get dressed quickly. I am hungry, as usual, and we are late for the Refectory.

Of my other, more terrible, secret I say nothing. As the days pass, everywhere I look I wonder if the women I saw with Amos on the beach are right here among us. I never saw their faces clearly. I want to pretend that I never witnessed what I saw, that such knowledge does not exist. But each time I smell the tobacco on Amos, I see that other Amos and her sudden yielding form in the arms of the enemy, her moonlit face uptilted to his. There was a kind of ecstasy to it, a kind of happiness that I have never seen, yet with a hot rush of some recognition, knew instantly.

Amos! Skinny, bald, dedicated, unsmiling Amos.

But I have to report something to the Prefects because that is what is expected after a walkabout, and I fear that my behavior will give me away if I do not tell them something. I rack my brains for some event to distract them, something that will not reveal my other secrets.

Something acceptable does come to me, slithering into my mind the way it slithered over the rock. They like to hear of new sightings, new animals. In fact it is obligatory to report such a sighting. There are so few creatures remaining from the teeming multitudes that must have supplied the people of the Time Before.

And I have one for them: the scaled thing that slipped over the rock and was gone.

"I need to report a sighting of a creature I cannot name," I say once I have found a Prefect. It just happens to be Underwood, the one who was chosen to beat Bayles. She gives a short, irritated sigh but nevertheless goes off to get the Ledger in which such sightings must be logged.

When she returns she makes me sit down at one of the long tables in the empty Refectory. She picks up the quill. "Start again," she commands. "What did it look like?"

"It was just a glimpse and it was dark. It gleamed a little, and it didn't have fur. It was like a kind of long fish, perhaps. But like one that can somehow live out of water."

"Did it make a noise of any kind?" The Prefect begins to write down my answers. The setting down of the words on the page is slow and labored because she is unused to writing.

"No. It was sliding. It didn't make any noise at all."

"Can you remember anything else?" She looks up. "It sounds like a mutant creature."

"I can't think of anything it could be. Perhaps it was a mutant."

She picks up the quill again. "There must be more. Think hard."

But it is all I have to offer. "It was too dark," I say. "I'm not even sure that I really saw it. Perhaps I was dreaming."

Underwood frowns. "I don't think you were dreaming," she says briskly. She reads over her own writing and taps the quill on the page. Then she tells me that I am dismissed.

Relieved, I think of it no further.

THE MILD, dry days come to an end and it has begun to rain. The Committee Members, wearing black cloaks that fall to the ground, come to survey us toiling in the fields. We must take advantage of the rain and the soft soil and plant as quickly as we can. The Committee Members stand beneath flimsy, spoked, dripping contraptions they call "umbrellas" and then they leave just as wordlessly, thinking their inscrutable thoughts and resembling a line of blackened scarecrows moving across the fields. No matter how long they are among us, we do not grow accustomed to them. The days pass in a routine of work and training and chores: the difficult to be practiced, the mouths to be fed, the dirt to be kept at bay, and the broken things to be mended. Day after day the rain falls with a soft insistence and we do nothing but work.

I am trudging about and so sorry for myself that I almost miss the announcement of a free hour before

Refectory this evening. At last! A chance to go to the Library and beg some pages, something to escape from this unending boredom.

When we are at last dismissed, I run through the rain and across the Quadrangle to the Library, hoping against hope that one of the Librarians is there to unlock the little cages on the shelves in which they keep the stacks of pages.

The tall red doors at the entrance are not locked but there does not seem to be any Librarian present. I am impatient and begin to tap my fingers on the counter behind which a Librarian usually stands, a bunch of keys on her belt, keeper of the imprisoned pages that might otherwise drift away.

The main thing I like about this room is that it is circular. The ceiling is a high dome and the walls soar upward. But this evening there is no time for gazing and I really want a Librarian to come. I do not care what she offers me. Any pages will do, so long as they are not about planting or weeding or watering anything.

My tapping turns to loud drumming and I even think to call out, which will be an impertinence, but one I must risk if I am to have my pages. I draw breath to do so but only the tiniest of frightened squeaks comes out.

She must have been standing there for some time but I had not seen her: Ms. Windsor. And she is wearing a skirt. The last light of the evening that spills from the dome gilds the outline of her form, but her face is in partial shadow. I cannot fully see her expression. My mouth has gone dry. I cannot speak. It is of no matter because she starts to speak instead, her words clear but clipped in a way that is unfamiliar to me.

"The Librarian, whom you are so eager to see, has gone to look for some pages that I requested. She shall return momentarily." Her skirt, which I now see is of a rich dark blue, swishes on the floor tiles as she takes a few steps toward me. I can see her face better now, the fine features that I remember from the day she lifted her veil, the day when she indulged in her whimsical sideways-riding. She is not wearing the yellow glass eye mask either, and her eyes are gray, cool, and intelligent. She even seems amused at this tall, awkward Novice still standing with her hand clapped over her mouth. I am taller than she is, and in comparison to her neat, contained shape, I feel myself to be all angles and elbows. She is close enough now that I can smell her, a sharp, delicate scent, something I cannot name until it suddenly comes to me: geraniums, their crushed leaves.

I let my hand drop to my side and bow my head in the way that is seemly in the presence of any authority. I should not have looked at her so directly or with such curiosity.

"In the meantime," she continues, "you could tell me what it is you were intending to read in your free hour. I understand that you are a keen reader. One day perhaps you may like to visit my private Library in Johns." She smiles a little. "Like you, I never really cared for chess or darts or mah-jongg." She pauses and looks wistful for just a fraction of a second, as though she were remembering something from long ago. "Those games always seemed absurd to me. Dry strategy, contingency, something about it that is too, what shall I say . . . bloodless? Yes, bloodless."

So shocked am I at this conversation that I have begun to shake. How does she know that I do not care for chess or mah-jongg? She and her Committee Members must be watching me. Why? I must be careful. I must be very careful.

She tilts her head and smiles. "So, tell me, what would you have the Librarian fetch for you when she returns?"

Looking down at the floor, I mutter something about not minding, that I like all the pages I am given, which is of course a convenient lie. All I want is to turn tail and run.

"Perhaps I may make a suggestion," she says, still with that smile in her voice. Then it drops to a low hiss. "Snakes," she says. "Serpents."

I take a step backward and she takes a tiny step

forward. "Are they not something fascinating? I could have the Librarian bring some pages on serpents."

For an instant the floor seems to tilt. I make no reply and instead look up. I will meet her eye. I am weary of hanging my head. If she wants to taunt me, or to punish me, then let her do it to my face. I hold her gaze and she returns it levelly. She is still amused, perhaps more amused at my small gesture of defiance. Her countenance, despite what she has just said, is not severe.

"You know," she says, and her tone is such that she sounds as if she were just idling her time with me, "I think by now, with all our dallying, you may have missed supper in the Refectory. I think it would be a good idea for you to eat, don't you? Once I have received my pages, I shall be returning to my quarters, where my supper will be brought to me. I could request an extra plate. So, would you care to join me, to dine with me? After all, you cannot go to bed hungry, can you? We could talk . . . and eat, of course."

Behind her there is a shuffling sound, and the Librarian bobs out of the shadows carrying a bundle of pages tied with string. It is the same white-faced Librarian who once mistakenly gave me the pages about the serpent in the garden. She must have confessed her error. I imagine her, flustered under the cool eye of Ms. Windsor, thumbing back through the

Ledger where I have entered my name over and over. My betrayer refuses to look at me and instead hands the pages to Ms. Windsor, with more nervous bobbing.

In a voice as loud and clear as I dare, making sure the Librarian can hear every word, I say: "Thank you for your kind invitation. I would most gratefully join you for supper."

CHAPTER NINE

THE LAMPS have already been lit when we enter the apartments that have been reserved for Ms. Windsor, and a small fire burns in the grate. There is a long green chair, upon which she invites me to sit.

"Sit on the couch," she says. I stroke it like a cat because that is what it feels like. "It's called velvet," she says. If I am indulging in Sensuality, she makes no attempt to admonish me.

Almost immediately, as if she had been waiting in some hidden alcove, one of the Housekeepers carries in a tray of food and sets it upon the table in front of the long chair upon which I am perched. When she enters the room and sees me, her nostrils flare in surprise like a startled horse. I believe she would have snorted if she had not managed to control herself. I will have to explain myself once this encounter, whatever it turns out to be, is over.

The food smells wonderful but I cannot see what it is. The plates are covered by domed silver lids, something I have never seen before. Ms. Windsor pulls up her own chair, a spindly thing with bowed legs. It doesn't look as if it could take even her slight weight. The richly colored skirt spills around her, fold upon fold, sometimes the color of deep, clear sea and other times the dense color of pine needles, depending on how the light catches it. She is so fragile a strong wind might snap her in two. Now that I am up close, I see that she is not as beautiful as we had all thought. Her features are too sharp, her skin is as thin as paper, and her eyes are rimmed with red, but she has refinement and poise that somehow trick the eye into seeing her as beautiful.

With a kind of delicate disgust, she leans forward and raises the domes on the food tray and peeks underneath each one.

"Well," she says dryly. "It's not the stallion, at least." She smiles. "He seemed to last forever."

I look hungrily at the domes but she does not offer to begin the meal. Instead she sits back, upright and composed but also relaxed, her shoulders level. As when she rides, she has perfect posture.

There is a short silence in which I cannot help but further study this room. There are two threadbare carpets on the floor, woven in intricate patterns that almost look like words or symbols. The fragile wooden chair upon which Ms. Windsor sits is one of a pair, placed on the other side of the table. There is another, plainer chair and a desk by the window, its leather top covered in Library pages tied with string, a chess set (despite her apparent dislike of the game), a few quills, an inkstand, and a jar of pencils. Her yellow mask lies there. A word is printed across the broad strap: ROSSIGNOL. Beside the mask is a timepiece of some kind, a found object that is bright orange, fat, and round. It stands on little legs with a kind of key at the back and it has a smiling, dimpled face around which the numbers are painted. My eye comes to rest upon the strangest thing of all: On a narrow table by the door there is a plant. But it is clear that it is not a real plant, because its leaves are made of some stiff, dusty fabric. There are even a few soiled blooms, also made of the same faded stuff, seemingly pinned to the lifeless stems and stalks of the sad thing. What could be the possible purpose of such an object?

There is a room beyond this main one. A canopied bed is just visible and Ms. Windsor's silver fur, something that I covet, has been spread across it. Does she feel cold at night? For an instant I see her, a slight figure lost in the huge bed alone under the weight of her fur, awaiting the oblivion of sleep. How lonesome does she get? Is she lonely like me?

The ceilings in both rooms are high. Despite the fire burning in the fireplace, this room, which I take to be that thing called a parlor, is quite chilly, and in some way quite desolate, even though the finest of the found objects have been used to furnish it.

"Do you get cold in here? And what is that un-alive plant for?" I blurt out these questions, my thoughts dropping straight from my head to my tongue.

"Oh." She glances at the plant and shudders with the refined distaste she showed before. "That thing. It's horrible, don't you think? I believe it is some form of Decoration. I don't know why they put it in here. Thought it would please me, no doubt."

She catches my eye because we both know that Decoration is forbidden, an unnecessary hindrance to the hard business of life. "A good thing that some Decoration is forbidden," she adds and smiles again, that small, tight smile. "Ugly things like that *shouldn't* be allowed. They do nothing to cheer the spirit."

What does she mean, "*some* Decoration"? *All* Decoration is forbidden, isn't it? Her voice is crisp, as if every thought were crystal-clear. But all she says in answer to my other question is: "Yes, I do get cold in here sometimes. Especially at night."

At long last she begins to lift the domes off the food. There is a single glass and a pitcher of water, fish stew, potatoes, cabbage, and a bowl of plums preserved in syrup, from I don't know where—I haven't seen plums for months.

She ladles out the stew, much more for me than

for herself, and I eat, trying not to devour it too quickly, although we are not used to holding back. We always attack our food, or so the Housekeepers say, but we get so hungry and there's never quite enough food to go around. Ms. Windsor picks at the stew and then places a spoonful of the plums in a bowl, setting it to one side as if saving it for later, something we would never do. She pours some of the water into the glass and takes a sip. The glass fascinates me. We always drink from thick brown clay mugs made in the potteries at Bareneed Farm.

"Eat the rest," she says, gesturing to the food as though she wishes it away, wishes it had never arrived. And then, with just the slightest spark of impatience, "We haven't had our talk yet." She makes me feel sweaty and effortful, a galumphing, gobbling embarrassment. I put my bowl down.

She goes over to the desk and picks up some of the bundles of pages, which she brings over. She sets the tray on the floor to make room for them and proceeds to select a few of the pages from one of the bundles.

"You see," she says, as though we were already in midconversation, "our weather is not what it was. It is bringing about all kinds of changes, ones that we cannot foresee." She sifts through the pages, apparently looking for some particular one. Her head is down and the lamplight shines on the crown of her hair combed so close to her skull. The scent of crushed geranium leaf hangs in the air around her.

"It used to be very cold here, cold for months and months; snow and ice covered the ground. But you know of our hot spells, of course. Things changed, you see, long ago. Sometimes new creatures come, which is why any sightings must be logged. And you did the right thing, Keller, telling Underwood about your sighting. These warm spells that bring the unknown creatures come and go, but the thing is, they never used to come at all, it seems. As you know, there have never been snakes in Foundland. Not ever." Her head snaps up and she looks me straight in the eye. "None."

I remain silent, the cat-velvet of the long chair-object pressed beneath my palms. She continues, turning away and looking into the gathering dark outside. Rain spatters the windowpanes.

"They need warmth, you see. They are cold-blooded and they need the warmth of the sun's rays to survive, to warm up their blood so that it can circulate around their bodies. And when they bite, their fangs are filled with terrible venom."

Her hand drops onto a page like a hawk dropping to its prey. She passes it to me. It is a page of images of long creatures with no legs and scales like fish, but with strong patterns in silver and brown, green and black. Their eyes are vacant and lidless; their heads are either flattened like an arrow pressed to the ground, or rounded and somehow incomplete. One has what must be a thread of a tongue that protrudes and is split in two.

"They are snakes," she says simply. "Have you ever seen one?"

I close my eyes and remember the slither of a brief, scaled thing over the rock. And the record of this sighting is in Underwood's Ledger. Is this why I am here in this chilly room with the Committee Chair? Is it a trick of some kind? Does she want me to tell her more? Does she want to lure me into telling her what I really saw the next night?

"Out on my walkabout, I saw something that could have been a snake. It slipped over the rock where I was settling down to sleep. It was not something with which I was familiar. But it was so quick, I barely saw it. Fish scales that were silvery, I think." If this is all she wishes me to disclose, then I'll have done with it and be dismissed.

And yet I don't want to leave. I am spellbound by this place and by being in the presence of this woman who is of so much fascination to us all.

"Perhaps it was a snake, then." I set the page with the images back down on the table and for an instant ponder whether or not to put it facedown. There is something that disturbs me about the creatures although they are also quite beautiful. I leave it faceup. Even unsettling images are worth contemplating.

There is a different silence now, an intent, listening silence. Ms. Windsor's whole body is tense and her eyes are shining.

"Those pages you read, the forbidden pages that that idiot Librarian gave you, they told you something about serpents, did they not? About a serpent in a garden that came to tempt a woman, Eve-woman, to eat an apple from the tree of knowledge. And when she did, she and the Adam-man, who was also in the garden with her, were banished to a cruel world. Her punishment was pain in childbirth and all kinds of evil was descended upon them and the earth. Did you read this?"

She sounds urgent now, needing the information quickly, but I am bewildered. I have no idea of what garden she speaks or these people, Eve-woman and Adam-man. Frantically I try to remember those pages, those lines. "I didn't read the whole story. I n-never do. The p-pages don't contain whole stories." I am stammering and now, to my horror, I can feel a tear that threatens to spill upon my cheek. I draw in breath and cling to the edge of the long green chair, willing the tear to retreat. But Ms. Windsor's voice has softened, dropped to another pitch. She is going to tell me a story.

"In Johns, where I live, I have my own large private Library. When you are a leader you can have such things, you know." She pauses. "Would you like your own Library, Keller? Shelves upon shelves of books, just for you and no one else?"

"I don't know," I whisper. What does she mean, "books"? The tip of her tongue touches her top lip. She continues with her story.

"Well, in that Library there is this book." She stops again to contemplate me, to make sure that I am attentive. "You know of books, do you not? Not pages, books. Books are pages that are bound together and then covered. They are beautiful objects."

"No," I say. In my mind I see the stacks of smooth, bound pages in the cavern, and the riot of images and the swarming words upon them.

"In the Time Before, this book of which I speak was an immensely powerful book. From this book, things were explained. All things. It was the book of man. This book was not a book of woman. In time, the book became less important but its power did not fall away altogether. The damage was done because in this book, it is said that it was woman who first engaged with evil, with temptation. It says that this serpent came to the garden and enticed the woman to eat fruit from the tree of knowledge. When she succumbed, she destroyed innocence and brought the knowledge of evil, of experience, to the world. The serpent is the symbol of temptation—you understand symbols, do you not?"

She looks at me sharply. "A serpent," she repeats. "This book says we are weak, capricious, curious, and meddlesome, and that we are to be subjugated, beaten, held prisoner if necessary, dominated. This book says everything is all our fault." She pauses to drink some more water, drains the glass and refills it, but does not drink. "Like children! They were treated like children." She spits out the words as if her patience has been tested to the limit. "But it is the book that is childish, the book that led to our subjugation."

I blink at the fury with which she says this. Her ranting is wearing me out and, after the salty stew, I realize how thirsty I am. But she does not offer me any of the water. What would she do if I were to reach out and drink from the refilled glass? I am overtaken by recklessness. I am in so deep now, I may as well drown. The water in the glass sparkles but I do not move my hand to it.

"Symbols are mighty things," she says. "This is why we must control them, symbols, images . . . and words." She is watching me, judging my reaction. "You like words a great deal, I understand. The written word. It is different, is it not, from the spoken? Has a power all its own." She draws breath and reverts to her storytelling.

"This book, the book of man, hid the real truth, of course. And the truth was this: The book was, in fact, saying something else. The book was full of fear, fear that was misdirected into convoluted stories. And do you know what that fear was?"

"No." I sound unexpectedly clear, even insolent.

"Fear of themselves! Fear of their own lust, male lust! And all laws, even after the power of the book fell away, the whole construction upon which the peoples from the Time Before based their communities, was built upon controlling and subjugating that devouring, screaming, ravening lust that dwelled in the breast of the male of the species. Given free rein, they knew it could destroy. It would be the life force that turns into the force of destruction. Men, you see, are tortured by their very own natures."

I stare at her. No one has ever told me so much about the Old People. I try to think back to some of the forbidden images we have seen in the hidden dwelling, the tiny, glossy women smiling from their pages, and the other ones that gaze into the distance at something only they can see. Their lives looked so happy and smooth. They didn't look as if they were being hunted down by lustful, tormented men at all. I almost open my mouth to say so until, with my heart knocking against my rib cage, I realize the stupidity of such a thing.

Ms. Windsor presses on. "Behind every move, every sin, and every act of violence, lies this lust, this life force that propelled the Old People toward disaster. It both terrified them and sustained them. They were clever, to be sure. Their greed and their lust were unparalleled. But once it was sated, it made them feel something else."

She picks up the page with snake-images and, with the tip of her finger, traces the outline of one of the creatures. "Yes," she murmurs. "You see, what it made them feel was something also very powerful." Then she stops, almost as if she were finished with her tirade. It has frightened me and yet, I am also pulled helplessly toward her and the terrible heat of her truths. It is as if, at this particular moment, the two of us are the last people alive in the whole world.

She continues to speak in her low voice. "It made them feel shame," she says. "And because of this, they felt the need to worship, to prostrate themselves before an imaginary power, an idol in the sky, to beg forgiveness and to give thanks. An idol that told them that women were lesser beings."

And then she flings both hands in the air as if in exasperation. "Have you ever heard of such absurdity?" She laughs, a long, low belly laugh that is so unexpected, I am startled into grinning. I know not where I am with this woman. She has me twisting and turning to her every mood.

"What a waste of time! Even the women asked for forgiveness on their behalf! They pleaded to nothing and no one." Her voice drops. "Idiots."

She grows solemn again. "So you see how the

women were denied? They provoked this lust, this life force. They were blamed for provocation, and they were blamed for the destructive power it unleashed. They could never win. But Tribulation came and granted us a new start and we have triumphed. We have eliminated this absurd story full of loathing and shame. How good it is that we are rid of this nonsense!" Then she does something terrible: She screams as one possessed. *"The women from the Time Before were powerless! Utterly powerless! Do you understand? I will never be powerless. I will never let that happen."* Her face has turned red and her lips are pressed into a thin line. In my terror and confusion, I almost leap and run from the room.

But as quickly as she had become upset, she composes herself. I hear footsteps in the passageway, the Housekeeper come to see if anything is wrong. She is waved away. The color drains from Ms. Windsor's face and her pallor returns. She places her hands in her lap, left gripping the right, which twitches with a life of its own. A thought occurs to me: Is she sick?

My own head aches. The familiar throbbing over my left eye has begun and is now so bad that I can't stand to look at any light, not that there is much of it now. It is fully dark outside and the lamps in the room offer only a few spots of sour light. The fire in the grate, which has not been tended, is dying and the room has grown even colder.

Ms. Windsor, after her story, if that is what it was, remains sitting very still. It is clear that she has not said all she wanted to say. She picks up the bowl of untouched plums, only to put it back down again.

"You see, if you ever find another serpent again, you must bring it to me, do you understand? You must trap it and bring it directly to me." She frowns and then says, "You look tired. I see you touching your temples. Do you have a pain there?" She reaches into the folds of her skirt and withdraws a tiny bejeweled box.

"Hold out your hand." I do so and she turns my hand over so that it is facing palm-up. From the box she tips some white powder into the center of my palm. "This powder kills all pain," she whispers. "Put it in your mouth and drink some of the water."

I do as I am told, trying not to gag on the bitter powder. She taps some of it into her own palm and puts her hand to her mouth. The tip of her tongue darts out to take up the powder in a movement so practiced that it seems part of her, the same way Amos rolls her cigarettes. She takes a moment and then says, "Have you ever thought how I came to be the Chair?"

The thought has never occurred to me. Our leaders just seem to be there, appearing in place as if they have always been there.

"No, I have not." There is an awkward silence, as

if I have said something rude, so I try to find something more to say. "Um . . . were you chosen?"

"Yes, you could say that. Initially, that is. It is perhaps the most important stage, getting picked out for your skills, an unswerving dedication, a clear head, and intelligence. Curiosity is useful but only up to a point. You see, what is needed is someone who can appreciate all sides of a problem. The leader is someone who can then pick one side. She decides; she commands without any further vacillation." Her hand slices the air. She shoots me a look but then continues.

"When this person is found, so begins the grooming process whereby you are placed in positions of greater and greater responsibility. But there comes a moment, and it is just that, *a moment,* where there is no one higher to do the choosing. Ultimately, what you do is choose yourself. You appoint yourself as the leader and make it so that others do not dare disagree. They cannot because you have made yourself so indispensable, so very necessary. *And, most of all, because you have decided it is to be.*"

Her eyes flash, the same exhilarated expression as when she lifted her veil the day she rode in that bizarre, pointless, beautiful fashion.

"Timing," she says. "That is how you become the Chair." She glances once again at the uneaten plums, the rare sweetmeat that she appears to disdain. She picks up her spoon, then lays it back down and instead drinks from the water glass. "But first, as you say yourself, you have to be chosen from the rank and file." She inclines her head to me. "Selected," she says. "I keep an eye out for the ones we can trust." She picks up the pitcher and empties it into the glass and hands it once more to me. "Drink," she says.

And before I do, I hold the glass up to the light. There is a mark upon its edge, a crescent, the shape of her lower lip, and it is a color, faint pink, an imprint of her mouth.

I know I am to leave but I have one question. I am compelled to ask it but already the powder is taking hold. I am floating and I must fight to get the words out in the right order.

"Why," I mumble. "Why did you ask me here to eat supper with you?"

"Oh." Her voice sounds tiny, as though it were coming from far away. "There were two reasons. The first is that you saw the snake and I had to hear about that. If there is a snake in our land, I must know. In fact, I should have been the first to know. You are a seer. You have the seeing eye, Keller. You must use it wisely." Her voice is fading now; I can hardly hear her as the words dissolve and recede. It is as if she is calling to me: "The other reason I asked you here for supper is because you, I think, are the only one who would dare ask the very question you just posed."

THE WHITE POWDER has had an effect such as I have never before experienced. I lie in my bed pain-free, relieved of my every burden. Would that I had such a powder in my own possession, just for me.

Due to my supper with Ms. Windsor, I have missed Inspection, and the Patrol members were already asleep when I came in. Proctor, the Prefect who is on duty tonight, watches me suspiciously as I undress and fall into bed.

"Why do your eyes look so funny? Your pupils are dilated."

I smile at her but I can't be bothered to reply.

She seems to know where I have been and does not press me.

"What did you have for supper?" I say, although it comes out as "shupper."

"Turnips."

"Turnips," I repeat in a singsong voice. "Turnips."

Images dance in my head: the orange timepiece with the numbers and the crazy smiling face; the bowl of untouched, glistening plums; the smell of crushed geranium leaf. And the images of snakes, the man and woman in the garden, the evils unleashed.

"Pandora," I murmur.

"What on earth is wrong with you? Shut up and go to sleep." Proctor blows out the candle.

And then I dream. All my limbs are loose and my skin is warm. A horse and rider are pounding toward me, and the rider is a man, not a woman. I can see the lather of sweat on the horse's flanks and the man's forearms, knotted with muscle and veins. But as they thunder closer the horse collapses, penitent and silenced, like the stallion I shot. The man-figure upon it crashes to the ground too. Before I can properly look at him, his form slips away from me. Then there is nothing, just vast, empty plain and a shimmer of the heat left behind from the man and the horse. Then darkness and I am gone.

CHAPTER TEN

GALLOPING MUST BE the greatest joy in the world.

The mare's hooves thunder over the ground and throw up clods of earth. Ryan, Pike, Carrow, and Laing are some way behind, but I can hear them yelling and laughing, trying to force yet more speed out of their animals. My mare is so fast that my eyes are streaming in the wind. My body feels light, fused with the horse and her power—there is nothing quite like it. When we reach the top of the hill, the mare's flanks heaving, I whoop as loud as I can and fling my arms around her neck, smelling the horseflesh, laying my cheek on her sweat-soaked neck. But once loosed from contact with the reins she drops her head to graze, ignoring my embrace. The others slow at the crest of the hill and then trot over to join me and the mare.

The weather is being kind. The crops we have

labored over all these days are growing, and there is a huge sense of relief. I had not realized how grave the situation was becoming. The Housekeepers have muttered about the cuts in their ration coupons. Our food stocks must be low (turnips for supper is a bad sign), although of course no one has said any such thing outright.

Today, Amos has told us to "go for a gallop," which she does on occasion when the mood takes her and we are to be allowed a treat. The sky is a huge blue bowl around us and the sun is warm, not the searing heat that may well follow in the days to come. We have brought bread and cheese to eat, so we dismount, run up our stirrups, and unbuckle the reins from the bridles so that the horses can graze. We sit down in the grass to have our picnic, shoving away the horses, who, once they realize we have bread, nose at our shoulders, pulling their soft lips back over their teeth.

"I am going to sunbathe," Laing announces. She pulls her shirt over her head and then her undershirt, so that her bare skin and breasts are exposed to the sun. She sits for a while self-consciously, then lies down and wriggles off the rest of her clothing apart from her underwear. Carrow, awkward but still faithful, does likewise, but the rest of us keep our clothes on. The breeze lifts our hair and from the top of the hill, the terrain is laid before us. We can make out a light mantle of green where the crops are beginning to show in the fields to the east. The Dwellings and the Stables, all of our little settlement, can be seen from here, as well as the larger mass of the College and the perfect square of the Quadrangle, demarcated by the straight lines and symmetry from the Time Before, the sure, unerring hand of the Old People.

"So what *else* did she say?" Laing sits up, an arm across her breasts.

I can tell she would like to put her shirt back on but her pride will not let her. The grass must be scratchy and a few red blotches have appeared on her back. She has been relentless in demanding details of my encounter with Ms. Windsor, pinning me down at every turn for more and narrowing her eyes as if she suspects me of withholding anything. In truth, I cannot remember every detail the way I would have liked, something I put down to the white powder she gave me.

"You want to hear it all over again?"

"I'll tell you when it starts to get boring," she says.

"She gave me some of that white stuff she takes, which made me float on a cloud. And she told me the story about the man and the woman in the garden, and the snake. She spoke some more about this book, about how it was a book of man. It made her so mad. She screamed that the women from the Time Before were powerless, all because of the snake, or something. It was very complicated."

As soon as I say the word *snake*, Pike chimes in. "There are no snakes here. There have never been snakes here."

Carrow too sits up. She is so thin that it is possible to count the ribs beneath her white skin. Her pale red hair is so fine that it seems to be hovering around her skull rather than growing from it. The bright sunlight makes her squint through her strange white eyelashes, and she is concealing her breasts with her arm, hunching over. She picks at a blade of grass.

"*Did* you see a snake? You never say, do you?" She pauses. "And why did she ask you to eat supper with her? I mean, why *you*?" It's a shaky challenge but a real one. "What makes you so special?"

"How would I know? Why don't you just go and ask her if you're that interested." I wait to see her reaction, but her head is still bent and she is still picking at the grass. "She says I have the seeing eye."

Carrow looks up, shielding the sun from her face with her long, white arm.

"And what is that supposed to mean?" She shunts a little to one side, turning her bony back to me. I want her to cover herself because I do not want to look at her meager white body.

"I saw those new birds," volunteers Pike. She has told us this before, months back. She had reported it with much solemnity, as is our way when we think we are being virtuous. "They hung in the air by beating their wings and they had long, curved beaks and were this tiny." She cups her hands as if she were holding one. "I had never seen them before. They were new, I'm positive. The weather—"

Laing is supremely uninterested in our nature findings and cuts her off before Pike has a chance to continue making her case about our ever-changing weather. "Tell me about the blue-green skirt again, how it changed colors." She lies back down in the grass, squinting at the sky. "And about the way she wouldn't eat her plums. And about her bedroom, and her fur. Tell me again about the way she smells of geraniums, and what her hands look like up close and the glass from which she drank and that pink mark left by her lips."

Her expression is alive as she conjures up these details for herself, without needing my words. Ditching her pride now, as if she has chosen the moment when it suited her, she slips her shirt back on and settles down in the grass.

"Tell me," she says. "One more time."

Carrow's back is still turned away from us. Her face is concealed, her head resting on her arms, which are folded over her knees. If I did not know better, I might think she was weeping, but of that there is no outward sign. We are all tightly trained in the art of controlling tears. Is it possible to weep inside?

I start up with my story as Laing luxuriates in it, captivated by me and my story. Carrow has no such story to tell, no such secret. Such is our currency, it would seem, and I have more of it now than Carrow.

"We're going to the place tomorrow," says Laing. "We're going to open the new door that Keller found. Are you coming, Carrow?"

Carrow looks up, her face stricken. "Of course I'm coming," she says. "Why did you need to ask? I always come." Her eyes are shining, brimming with tears. She turns her face away again.

"Oh," says Laing lightly. "I just thought perhaps you had become tired of it."

LAING CANNOT WAIT to get inside. "Find a claw hammer and pull those planks off so we can get in." Her whole frame is tense with anticipation. "Why didn't you go in when you could have?"

I do not care for her orders so I do not answer but instead stomp up the flight of steps that leads to the door and yank at the nails with a crowbar. In minutes the door is opened, just a rectangle of dark space that leads to a beyond of more darkness.

I am the closest to the new entrance, but Laing, without any hesitation, squeezes past me. She carries no candle, and for all she knows, there could be nothing but a drop down into some black hole of nothingness. But then her voice, just a few feet away and just as imperious, commands us.

"Bring the candles. Everybody inside. Quick."

One by one we file in and light up a room that, even though it is all so jarring and unfamiliar, is obviously some kind of kitchen. Pots and pans hang from a rack above a wood-burning stove with a large griddle and the letters AGA embellished upon it. There are closets and two sinks, and a complicated faucet that begins as a single metal stem and then divides into two.

"It's a kitchen," squeaks Pike.

Carrow grips Laing's arm in fear or else in some attempt to restrain her, but Laing is surging forward anyway. "I think you're right, Keller," she says. "It is a dwelling of some kind."

Carrow's eyes are wide with wonderment and she stays as close as she can to Laing. She points to yet more doors, two of them, that are shut but have not been boarded up.

"There must be more rooms."

And I see why I always think the cavern is such a prison. There are windows, the panes of glass visible from the inside, but they are boarded up on the outside so that no light has penetrated this space for hundreds of years. Tendrils of vine curl through any crack and on the outer shell of boards and brick. There must be a thick, green living barrier hiding this place from the world. No wonder no one has ever seen it.

And I also know why I feel this overwhelming sadness when I am inside it. It should have been a place of life, and yet there is no life here. Just dead objects one after another, too strange, too many to name, in rooms that once must have held voices, the smell of cooking, maybe laughter, maybe song.

Wordlessly we drift through the rooms, a whole dwelling tucked so deep into the hillside that it is completely hidden, apart from the windows that long ago must have looked out on the surrounding lands down to Bareneed Farm. And now, after all these years, the vegetation has grown and grown, creeping over the bricks and the glass and the roof, as if the very earth itself were taking it back.

At each room, we pause to discern the purpose. There is a room that is a tiny latrine and another that we figure is a mudroom, from all the pegs and a few moldering boots in a pile. In the room that must have been a parlor, there are two of the excessively long chairs such as I had seen in Ms. Windsor's parlor, and several other soft chairs with small tables at their sides. There is a kind of soft covering on many of the floors, thick with dust. It muffles our footsteps, accepting our feet in a way to which we are entirely unaccustomed. In fact nothing is hard at all; all is cushioned and patterned with flowers and spirals of other colorful shapes—pink, brown, green, color whirling as in a dream, but a dream where all the images are obscured by cobwebs and dust.

Attached to one of the walls is a large, flat panel of gray glass that looks like a pointless kind of window because it reveals nothing. Beside it is a set of shelves that are mostly empty apart from some slim boxes in a row. There are words on the boxes, words that mean nothing to us: *Charlie and the Chocolate Factory, Annie Hall,* and *Terminator.* The chairs in the room are arranged so that they face the gray window, as if there were some special reason to sit and look at it.

There is Decoration at every turn. Even a fire screen made of orange metal is decorated with an image of a monster with an exceedingly long nose, huge flapping ears, and long, curved teeth that protrude on either side of its face. The screen has fallen on its side. Too scared to touch it, we leave it where it is.

On shelves there are many animals made of fired clay, glazed and decorated with refinement that we have never seen. We cannot name them all, but we do spy a pair of upright dancing pigs. They are each wearing little blue jackets, and their lower halves are unclothed and have no teats or genitals.

We creep down a long, shadowy passageway, opening first one door and then the next. There is a line of them, five in all, two on the left and three on the right.

The doors lead to what must be the sleeping quarters of the dwelling, for there are beds in each of the rooms, except for the one we name the Bath House, because it must be where they washed. The walls are tiled in dark blue and there is a kind of long tub streaked with rust. There is a stained lavatory, just like the ones in our own Bath House that we cannot use, and another kind of tiled closet with a rusted pipe leading to a metal head punctured with holes, also like the ones in the Bath House. We imagine water once gushed from them. It must have been like standing in the rain, except indoors.

But the most incredible thing about this small Bath House is that there is an enormous looking glass on the wall and over the two basins, which have divided faucets similar to those in the kitchen.

Laing leans over the basins and uses her sleeve to wipe clear an arc of silver in the dust, and we gasp as we see ourselves with such terrible clarity. We are transfixed. Working more vigorously with her sleeve, she rubs the whole looking glass clean. The motes of dust float up like midges, but we pay no mind to anything now other than what we can see in the mirror. It is entirely different from our rippling reflections in water pools or even in a pane of window glass. This glass returns to our gaze an exact likeness that both shocks and excites us.

We place all our candles around the basins so that

the glass is as brightly illuminated as possible and we jostle for space, touching our own likenesses on the smooth silver and marveling as each action we make is faithfully copied. We begin to pull faces and touch the likenesses of one another on its surface, shouting "Look at me!" and "Look at you!" over and over. Laing and Carrow begin their hip-wiggling dancing, rolling their eyes and tossing their hair, and soon we are all flinging ourselves about, one eye always on the looking glass, shouting and laughing as if we had never heard of the very first Pitfall: Reflection. And then I remember a scrap of something from one of the pages. Was it part of a story or was it code for something?

Mirror, mirror, on the wall. Who is the fairest of them all?

I whisper it at first and then I say it louder: "It's called a mirror." I shout over their excited yelping.

I have turned away from its pretty silver surface as quickly as I can. I saw my coarse hair, my dark worried eyes, and my wide, unlovely mouth.

Who is the fairest of them all?

Not me.

At the end of the passageway is a door. Upon it two words say DAYNA'S ROOM.

It is easy to see straightaway that it is another sleeping space, because in the center of the room is a lilac bed covered with pillows. Poles at each corner of the bed support a canopy that covers the bed like a sagging roof. It looks more like something that might be part of a ceremony than a place for the mere act of sleeping.

There is a skitter of rats in the shadows. Brambles of dog roses and tendrils of the vines and other vegetation that must cover the whole dwelling have crept through cracks in the walls and pushed their way through any crevices in the ceiling, dangling down or growing up the walls, quiet and relentless, from the living earth beneath. Lengths of vine have twisted around and over the poles that support the bed's canopy.

My candlelight flickers over the other objects in the room. There is a desk with a white box upon it. Encased by the box is another of the flat panels of gray glass, similar to the panel in the parlor, although not as large. Attached by a kind of string to this box is a flat board divided into little squares and, once I have wiped away some of the dust, upon each square a letter is revealed. The letters are in no proper order at all, and there are many signs or letters that I have never seen before. It is possible to push the squares down and they spring back up to their original position. When pressed, there is a faint clicking sound.

So absorbed am I with this object that I nearly jump out of my skin when I hear Laing's voice. She enters the room and her candle adds light so that we can see more. At each breath, the candle flames flutter and our shadows flee across the vine-covered walls.

Our light falls upon a row of small, false animals on the window ledge, deviant-looking bears and puppies and a blue rabbit. They have glass eyes that are covered in a film of dust, but no claws or teeth. Next to them are three identical little metal girls, each one set upon a black stand. The tiny girls are all frozen into a running position, their arms held out from their sides. Their heads are cocked to one side and they each have one leg poised, about to kick a little golden ball that balances on the edge of the stand. Their hair is about regulation length and tied in a ponytail, and they wear peculiar short trousers, long socks, and boots. Up close I can make out some letters that have been etched upon a strip of metal nailed to the little black stand. I say them aloud as best I can, although they mean nothing: "Goose Bay Girls' Soccer League."

On a little table by the bed is some kind of lamp, clothed with a frilled hat that sits upon a ball of glass so fine that we dare not touch it. It is tied to the wall by a kind of string. Clothes, or perhaps just rags covered in thick dust, lie in heaps on the floor, as do shoes and boots that have been scattered everywhere. Images on paper have been attached to the walls, but we cannot see what the images are because of the dust.

"It's a room for a girl," says Laing. Her voice trembles. "A girl like us. A girl from the Time Before." The others creep into the room.

Laing goes over to the bed and lies down. Her silver hair is spread across the pillows. Ivy and thorned brambles that have crept over the canopy trail over the edges, seeking purchase upon another surface. The room smells of an ancient, stale sweetness. Laing composes herself, closes her eyes, folds her hands upon her chest, and then just lies there breathing evenly. The rest of us gather around, looking down upon her. We are hesitant and uneasy, a mute feeling that we too should be doing something, performing some kind of role, but what that would be eludes us.

WE GO BACK to the hidden dwelling again and again. We flit through the night like moths past the slumbering Prefects, not even waiting until Bayles is on duty. It seems easy now. We run through the Quadrangle and out to the river, up the ridge, and then vanish into the hillside where the house is hidden by Nature herself. Our fear of the hidden dwelling subsides a little more with each visit, although it never entirely disappears. What we are doing is so very wrong. But we are entranced by the vine-hung, empty rooms full of soft chairs and even softer beds, and by the mirrors on the walls. We are especially entranced by Dayna's Room.

We take turns lying on the lilac bed that yields

clouds of moldy dust no matter how often we lie upon it. We turn Dayna's possessions over and over in our hands, the little metal girls that are always about to kick the balanced balls but never do, the lifeless animals on the window ledge, and a set of pipes hanging on strings that make a lost, sad chiming sound when we touch it. In the little table by the bed, pushed to the back of a drawer, we find a box of what are unmistakably cigarettes. But they are perfectly formed and nothing like the lumpy things Amos rolls for herself. The perfect cigarettes crumble to pieces beneath our fingers.

When we wipe away the dust on the paper images on the walls, some fall and disintegrate. There are some very small images of what looks like a cat wearing some kind of bonnet, asleep inside a box, and beneath those, a few more images of what must have been the people from the Time Before, but they are so creased and faded that no matter how hard we look, we can only make out the pale patches of their limbs and faces. Some of the larger images on the wall reveal themselves to be pictures of the shining women and the men-children in the slender books that we also find in piles on the floor. "Hot Guys!" it says over the images, but we do not know how to say the word *guys*.

"That must be what they were called," says Carrow. "The men-children in the images."

But it still doesn't quite answer our question as to

whether they are men or not, for the word makes no sense to us.

We don't spend much time reading the slender books because there is so much else to do, and the words do not help us anyway. Laing finds her "new" words, but it is as if the words are some other kind of language only half-familiar to us, a code that we may in time crack but that is impregnable to us now. "Are models and celebrities too thin?" they say. And "Summer's laid-back pieces make the living easy." We look to the images for help but mostly they do not help us. One woman has a bubble coming out of her mouth with the words: "Tonight I'm gonna put on fake eyelashes, eat a whole chocolate cake, and do nothing else except shop the meanest handbag sites on the Web. Ohmigawd! I feel guilty already!" The words mystify us, as do the people from the Time Before. They all sound so puzzlingly, enduringly happy.

There must have been some misery. "Date rape—how likely is it to happen to you?" they say. "Is sex education the only way to stop teen pregnancy?" and "My boyfriend beat me." Were those smooth men-children called *boyfriends*? Did they beat them? Were they friends? The women from the Time Before were raped, they were impregnated, they were beaten. This we knew. But we cannot know their world. We cannot know them.

There do not seem to be any images of women

doing any work. Sometimes there is an image of one who looks as if she may have gotten her hands dirty from time to time, one who looks tired or fat or used up. We have seen some images where the women are covered from head to toe in black, even their faces, which are imprisoned behind little mesh grilles from which they peep. These women must be in some form of mourning garb, we have decided, with their faces covered so that no one may see the shame of their tears.

Surely someone must have done the work, brought in the harvest, tended the livestock, and sewed the clothing, as well as all the dreary daily scrubbing and tidying. And something or someone must have made all the objects, the shoes and the colored, glimmering metal carriages in which the people sit, and the tiny, slender silver boxes they hold to their ears. Could they not hear properly? Did the box provide some kind of assistance? They hold them in their hands and study them intently.

In our hidden treasure trove, we have found there is something else, something that explains the images in some way, the eyes and glossy lips of the women.

The colors on their faces must be painted on because we find a cloth bag in the Bath House–type room that is full of paints and powders. Laing tells us it is these that make the women in the images so beautiful and so puzzling. Once we have opened the bag, which is cunningly fastened by a row of metal teeth, we find within many small metal cylinders with sticks inside, all in shades of pink and red.

"They're made of wax," says Laing quietly. "But they've turned hard." She warms the wax sticks with her candle flame. When they are soft, we smear the pigment onto our fingertips. There are also tiny blackened brushes inside slender cylinders. Laing spits on one of the brushes and wipes it across her palm, leaving a black streak.

"What are those little brushes for?" I am at a complete loss to explain them.

Laing hesitates, contemplating the object for a while, then she says slowly, "Eyelashes. You put it on your eyelashes. Or perhaps your eyebrows."

"Why?"

"I don't know," she says and spits on the brush again.

There are black pencils and circular boxes of silvery-blue stuff that has hardened until we crush it into a powder fine as soot. There are little bottles of flesh-colored paint, all manner of things that will make us look like one of the people from the Time Before.

Laing takes one of the little pencils and draws a thick outline around her dark blue eyes.

When she is finished, I gasp. "All these Pitfalls!"

"All these Pitfalls." She widens her eyes as she mimics me. "Stop being so lame."

She is transformed, wicked and exciting, no longer quite human in some way, as if she has put on a mask. She parts her lips and runs the broken stick of wax, blood-red, over them. The color smudges around the lines of her real lips and they look swollen, as if someone has beaten her. She tilts her face to the mirror, oblivious to my presence now, lost in her own painted image. When I touch the paint it is greasy and clings to the skin. A shudder of revulsion runs down my spine.

"Who is the most beautiful?" she asks.

I can feel her hot breath on my cheek and I step back from her, suddenly terrified. Her face makes me remember something that we had found in another room.

On our last visit we found a box in Dayna's Room. It was at the back of a closet, covered by a heap of clothes, and was full of tiny women made out of some kind of resin. They had long, long hair and they offered up breasts with no nipples. The place between their legs was as smooth and hard as the rest of their bodies. The shape of their feet went some way toward explaining how the women from the Time Before wore their shoes; they were indeed permanently on tiptoe. There was a frozen pink expression of incomprehension to their faces, wide eyes, and open mouths. One wearing a tiny crown had a silken sash across its body that said "Beauty Queen."

Also in the box were tiny clothes for them, although many of the women in the box were naked. There were some pieces of furniture and a horse wedged in upside down. Its mane was identical in texture and length to the hair of the women. The limbs of both the women and the horse moved stiffly and they could not stand upright by themselves.

We had no idea what these tiny pink women and their possessions were for. They lay there doing nothing, and it was as if we wanted to breathe some of our life into them. They frightened us. All of us, that is, except for Laing, who wanted to take them out and look at them longer. But after a while, even she agreed to put them back in their box and close the lid.

But now, as she gazes at herself in the mirror, she declares, "I want to be a beauty queen. We must have a contest to see who is the most beautiful. Everyone must come, everyone in the whole Patrol."

"I don't want to be part of your competition," I tell her. "It's a terrible, mean idea. The objects are beginning to scare me. We should stop coming here."

I was not telling her the whole truth. Part of me yearns to join in, but I have seen myself in the mirror: I am ugly. I cannot take part in a competition of beauty.

And yet I am ravenous to know this new world of shining, gorgeous women. We all are. We have become raiders of the dwelling and all the objects within it. We fight over the bowls and boxes full of jewels and tiny metal chains as well as delicate, dangling, hooked objects that often come in pairs. By studying the images, we figure out that the hooked objects were to be hung from the ears of the people from the Time Before. Did they bleed each time they pierced their earlobes in order to adorn themselves with these things? We hold them up to our own ears but do not try to force them through the flesh of our earlobes. Greedily, we pull things from closets. We go through the mounds of clothes that are heaped on the floor, the bags and sacks of many different colors, and we play with the shoes that are everywhere: shining, colored shoes with the blunt spikes that hang from the heel; shoes made of cloth, of leather; and the ones with thick, gridded soles that look as if they are for gaining traction on all the smooth surfaces of the Time Before.

We like the spiked shoes the best and we totter about in them, pretending to be in agony, shrieking with laughter because not a living soul can hear us. When we race home again through the night we stop at the river, and with handfuls of cold water, we scrub the paint off our faces so that we may return as pure and unsullied as when we first set out.

CHAPTER ELEVEN

THE BIRCH FOREST is cool and full of fugitive light as the breeze ripples through it. I long to just lie down and fall asleep on the forest floor—I am still tired from the previous night's revelry in the hidden dwelling. Smith walks in front of me. It was her suggestion to come to the forest instead of doing what I was sent to do, which was to help clean up her yard.

"Go and make yourself useful over there," Amos had said after it was discovered that my horse was lame and I would not be able to ride that day. Her order for me to work for Smith was puzzling. There were plenty of other horses I could have ridden. Was she sending me deliberately?

Smith is just ahead of me, making her way toward a small stand of ash trees in a dell that is set apart from the taller birch trees. "Ash is good for spokes," she says, and murmurs on about different kinds of wood. I am too sleepy to concentrate until she says something so casual and yet so shocking that I stop in my tracks.

"How's your ankle doing?" She doesn't even wait for a reply, just walks on as cheerful as usual, poking and prodding at the trunks of the trees and squinting up into their branches, assessing how much work felling and dragging back the timber is going to be.

How is your ankle doing? Not once had I limped when I returned from my walkabout. I have been so careful not to show any sign of pain or weakness—so how does she know about my ankle? There is only one possible answer, and that means she knows my darkest secret. She knows what I have witnessed. Was she there? Or did Amos tell her? Has Amos known all this time that I was there?

The forest reels around me and I can't get my breath. All of a sudden, I am wide awake. It is as if she has delivered me a blow. And here she is, whistling and making small talk. She marks the trees with her knife, the bark opening up to reveal the white fibers beneath, moist despite the heat and the dryness everywhere else. The smell of the sap is vital, and somehow calms my fears.

"How did you know about my ankle?" I have to call out because she is up ahead of me. "How did you know? Who told you?"

She turns and puts her finger to her lips. "Shhh," she says. She walks a bit farther on and when I catch up to her, she still ignores my question. "There is nothing more here I want to mark," she says. "I'm hungry now, anyhow. Let's go back into the coolest part of the forest and eat." She is looking at me in a strange way and it is clear that I am not to repeat my question, still less yell it across the forest.

She sits down beneath one of the larger trees. She is someone who can work for hours and hours, but she can also rest in an utterly complete way.

"Smith," I begin tentatively. "Have you ever seen something that moved on two wheels only?"

Smith sits up but not because she is particularly surprised. Instead she is rummaging in her pack for her tobacco. "You mean," she says, "like a kind of loading trolley with two back wheels, one that you pull with a handle?" She finishes rolling the cigarette and lights it. The smell of the cigarette smoke stings the back of my throat and yet, in some way, it is reassuring. I wonder what it would be like to smoke a cigarette.

"No," I say. "Not a trolley." I search again for words to describe the object that had caught my eye and made me wonder what Smith might have made of it. "The wheels are in line with each other and quite big."

Then I'm at a loss as to how to tell her. An unfamiliar urge overwhelms me. The only way I can think of is to make an image. I pick up a twig and brush aside a few leaves, and on the patch of soil I make a mark.

It is the strangest feeling, a kind of compulsion, the only way I can think of to tell her of the puzzling object. As I scratch in the soil I continue to talk, heedless now, and so eager.

"And in between, there is a triangle of metal. And there is some kind of seat and things that must propel it forward, upon which I think you place your feet. The wheels look quite similar to our wheels, with spokes, but they are not made of wood. They are made of metal and that stuff we sometimes find. I think it is called rubber. It must move and someone or something must sit upon the seat, and yet it is impossible to understand how one could sit on it without falling off. They must have had a different sense of balance from us in the Time Before. . . ."

The words tumble from me and I start to think of all the other baffling things I have seen in the hidden house and the square cavern, all the other things I want to describe and ask about.

Smith has become uneasy but I keep talking and talking: I cannot help myself. Then she suddenly extends one leg and in an instant kicks leaves and soil over my scratchings on the earth. She lays one of her fingers across my lips.

"Be quiet now," she says. "The trees have ears. And eyes." She raises her eyebrows as if to indicate a presence in the trees. "They watch us all, you know. Someone may be listening."

And then I am frightened. What have I said?

"It was something I saw in the pages," I say. "Sometimes the pages have images on them. I know we're not supposed to look. . . ."

"Come." Smith heaves herself to her feet. She unfastens the axes that are strapped to her pack and hands one to me. "It's best to get to work. Come on! Let's get going!"

She tramps off toward the stand of ash trees that she has already marked for felling, hoisting her pack onto her broad back as she goes, so purposeful and unhurried, and once again I am comforted just by being in her company, as if she can protect me from anything in the world. Perhaps this is what it feels like to be loved, I think, but the thought flees before I can pin it down. I scramble to my feet and follow Smith.

She has already begun to chop one of the bigger saplings. She does not pause but at each blow she times her questions. And over the blows I tell her, not everything, but a great deal about the square cavern, the house, the objects, the sadness of the place, about Dayna's Room. I do not mention the beauty queen competition. The thoughts of it still make me shameful and full of dread.

"And it seems that the people from the Time Before who must have lived there left in a rush," I say. "They left behind their objects. Perhaps they had many more that they took with them. But then, where did they go? The fire must have rained down upon them and the toxic cloud must have poisoned them . . . they can't have gotten very far."

"I don't know how," says Smith, "but the Committee Members must have gotten wind of this, which is why, among other reasons, they are staying here so long." She delivers a final blow and motions for me to step back as the sapling falls in a shiver of green and silver.

"You have discovered something that they have long suspected, long sought after, but have been unable to find." She hefts the ax from hand to hand and then I see that her face, though covered now in sawdust and leaf debris, is also lined with worry.

"You see, my dear, what I think you and Laing have found . . . is the first house in the Gated Community."

"What's the Gated Community?"

"It's become part of legend now. They've been looking for it for years. As you know, we haven't had a good find for so long and that is because there is almost nothing left *to* find. But there has always been talk of a big group of houses, filled with possessions from the Time Before. Imagine the treasure! And imagine how badly we need it."

"The things in this place," I begin. "I mean, I don't even know if I like it there. I don't know if we do need those sorts of things all that badly." But now that she is telling me so much, I must return to the thing I most need to know. Time is running out. I take a deep breath.

"There is something more, Smith, something else I have seen. You must tell me the truth. I have been so confused I think I'm turning crazy. On my walkabout, I saw Amos . . . she was on a hidden beach with—"

And then Smith's expression changes and she clams up. She steps over to haul at some branches, whipping them about to make more noise. A figure appears from the forest interior, a familiar figure limping into the sunlight of the dell where the felled ash trees lie. As she comes closer I catch the whiff of fish meal. It is Gosse, my Confidante. As she gets closer, she smiles and holds up her hand in greeting.

"Finally caught up with you," she says to me, ignoring Smith. "We haven't spoken in the longest time."

I CAN'T SEE how Gosse could have once been a Tracker. She limps and she sniffs and is such a weakling. And she smells of the salmon pools where she does her work. She takes me out of the forest without even looking back at Smith. When I turn around, Smith, sweaty and covered in wood chips, looks frightened. She tries to mouth something to me, but I am too far away to understand what she is saying.

Gosse tries in her usual uncertain way to be

friendly, but the walk back to the Dwellings is punctuated with awkward silences. "I think the rain is coming," she says.

Banks of clouds have been building in the afternoons, only to disappear by the evening. So far there has been no rain. The flies that had not bothered me when I was with Smith now buzz around our faces, forcing us to continually swat them away. The air has become oppressive.

"And this time it will rescue the crop," she continues. "Things are going to get better, so you must not despair."

She is lying: I know the stocks are low. I know that soon there will not be enough food. The portions on our plates are becoming more and more meager.

"There has been such despair, don't you think?" says Gosse. She really does want me to like her and trust her.

"I heard the Chair asked you in for supper. You were selected. That must have been . . ." She genuinely does not know what to say. The event, my sitting and partaking in a private meal with the very Chair herself, is such a rare occurrence that I am certain Gosse is as curious about the whole evening as everyone else has been.

"Yes," I say flatly. "We ate together. Stew. Potatoes. Plums." It is a cruel reply, offering her nothing.

"Plums? Oh my!"

We trudge on down the dusty track that not so long ago had been covered in snow bearing the sledges and the Committee Members.

"Do they have Seed with them?" I ask, trying to distract her.

"Seed?" She sounds shocked. "Oh, I wouldn't know about that. They would never say, even if they did. But . . ." She pinches the bridge of her nose with her forefinger and thumb. "But if they did, I can't quite see how they would keep it alive."

This time it is my turn to be surprised—and curious. What does she mean, "keep it alive"? Seeing my puzzlement, she looks even more doubtful as to the permissibility of this information. But she also knows that she has to give me something if I am to give her whatever it is she is after (and what that is, I am never sure). Her expression reveals a short struggle as she decides which way to go. "I m-mean . . . this heat. To keep it alive they need deep cold, the deepest there is. It's . . . it's a problem. Seed is . . . something of a problem at the moment. Never enough to go around. But, you know, we'll solve it one way or another. As we always do."

"Where do they get it from?"

"Oh, it is kept in the Bank, in Johns. They keep it deep in the earth, inside a seam of permafrost that keeps it cold at all times. It was in storage in a building, one of the miracles that was found from the Time

Before, but after a while, we had to find our own way of keeping it cold. Just one of the many lessons we have learned. But things change. There are things we cannot always control."

She stops for a few seconds. I can see that she is starting to tire. Her limping through the forest must have been too much for her, although she did quite a good job of not being seen. How much did she see or hear?

"Why did the men go? Why didn't they stay?" I know we have been told answers to these questions, but I am hoping I have caught her off guard so that she will tell me something new, which, of course, she does not.

She sighs. "They went away to war. Tribulation came. The few who returned were sick and crazed and contaminated." She looks at me almost sadly. "It doesn't matter now, does it? It was all so long ago." I can see she wants to change the subject. "So, you seem to spend a great deal of time with Laing."

"We don't have friends," I drone. "We are pure. We are one unit, the Patrol. Seeking out individuals is divisive and unnecessary. We are unified in arms. We are unified in our mission to heal the earth after the Tribulation brought about by the Old People."

"Ah," she says. "I see."

As we reach the top of the ridge she stops for a moment's rest and gazes across the valley. "Laing is quite an unusual girl, I think. Very powerful, in her own way."

I too look out across the valley. Heat shimmers over the dying fields.

Gosse gives me a sidelong glance. "She even has power over the Prefects. Well, one of them at least."

"Who?"

"Bayles," she says, and there is a light in her eyes now. She knows she has hooked me. "Do you know why she had to endure the Silent Beating?"

Never has a conversation so suddenly entered the realm of something so forbidden. Not even my image-making in the soil, right in front of Smith, bears comparison with what Gosse is about to do. To tell the reason behind a Silent Beating is a transgression of the grossest kind. I cannot believe that she will do it. Or why. But she keeps on talking.

"Yes. Bayles. You see, Bayles was smitten with Laing, with her being so beautiful and all. She tried to kiss her." Now in the midst of her revelations Gosse is speaking without hesitation. Her voice has turned hard and purposeful. "So Bayles had to be punished."

She ends it simply, as if she were merely relaying facts that have no real portent or consequence. "But she did the right thing. She confessed her misdeed and accepted her punishment." She pauses. "Power over people has many forms, does it not?"

My mind races back to each night we have escaped

from the Dormitory, each night we have visited the hidden dwelling. For once a mystery solved—by a betrayal. On so many of the the nights we went out, it was Bayles who was on watch. Bayles who, in some act of love, let us pass. Bayles who suffered the beating for Laing and who suffers her indifference, except for when Bayles became useful. What was she offered in return? A fleeting embrace? We are barely allowed to touch one another, let alone kiss! And I can almost see Laing laughing at her, shoving her away in disgust. And Bayles, stumpy, lovelorn Bayles, rejected, tending her wounds yet still hoping for . . . what? Love?

Gosse seems to be enjoying my confusion. "Is Laing your friend?" she asks again. Her voice is soft and persuasive.

"We are one," I say. "The Patrol is one." But my flushed cheeks and shaking hands have given me away. Gosse halts again and I see that by now she is probably in some actual pain with her leg. She gazes out over the valley, her eyes following the flight of a gull that has flown this far inland.

"Do you think you would have liked to be a Wheelwright?" It isn't a casual question. I look at her mutinously. Is it a veiled threat?

"No," I answer. "I am a Tracker. That is what I want." I fear demotion; I don't want to end up like Gosse.

"Yes," she says softly. The rooftops of the

Dwellings are in view now and I almost want to run the rest of the way just to get away from her. She lays a restraining hand on my arm. And in her eyes I see the disappointments of her own life, the way she has been relegated to the edges, the margins of things, where she can only watch and try to make her contribution.

"The trouble is, Keller, we can't always have what we want." She releases my arm and again her voice turns hard. "We must hold together if we are to live, to go on with our mission and atone for the sins of the Time Before. We must hold fast."

CHAPTER TWELVE

THE AIR SMELLS of apples.

A day after that hot, dusty trudge with Gosse, suddenly everything is cooled. The soil has received a downpour, delivered at last by the clouds that have been sailing in and out each day.

We assemble in the Hall to give thanks. We wear our white shifts and tie our hair back away from our faces. Bowls of apples, from the last of the stores, are carried in by the Prefects and the apples are solemnly handed out one by one to each of us. And so the Festival of Thanks begins. We hold our apples in our hands and take a single ceremonial bite. The Headmistress bites hers and then hands it to the Prefect who stands beside her at the lectern.

She waits until we have swallowed the mouthfuls of our fruit and then raises her hand to command the Sing.

We begin, the note rising and rising to a purity that seems to cleanse our very souls and to purge us of everything, even thought. The rain beats down on the hard earth outside. Soon it will yield and the plants will come green. We can begin once again to renew our bonds with the earth that were torn asunder by the Old People in ways we do not understand and can never know. How did they die? How did the few who survived get away? How did Dayna die?

I have tried to imagine what Dayna looked like but I have failed. I see her shape in the clothes in her wardrobe and we can feel the indentations of her feet in her shoes; once we found a single long, dark hair threaded through the fibers of a garment. We can play with the trinkets and the colored animals and the face paint, but she is known to us only through her possessions. And they are not enough. They do not let us truly see or hear or understand her. I close my eyes and breathe deep in order to lift my voice to the next note and to the next.

Ms. Windsor has taken over the lectern. She raises her small hand and the Sing ceases. When she speaks, her voice moves thin and high into the sudden silence.

"The rain has come and we have eaten of the apple," she begins. "We are sustained by it and protected. We Foundlanders will save ourselves and replenish this earth. Look what we have done with what we have. Our orchards, our fields, our unviolated borders. We have built a world for ourselves against all adversity. We have survived Tribulation for generations. We have rid ourselves of all deviants, the deviant men who would have otherwise ruled us. We have foiled attempts by the enemy to invade our territories, the enemy who would penetrate and subdue us, extinguish our very being. Be proud, my women! Be proud! We alone have been charged with healing the earth!"

She raises both her arms. The hectic spots of color rise on her cheeks, and her eyes glitter. As we raise our own arms, the apples in our right hands held aloft, we begin the Sing once more. She bows her head and her hand moves to some hidden pocket in her shift. Her finger, laden with white powder, moves with such grace, such speed as she puts the powder to her lips. She flings back her head, eyes closed, waiting for the notes to rise in her throat.

"Where do you think she gets it?"

Laing, who is next to me, looks ahead with her lips parted as if she is still in the Sing. She murmurs again. "That white powder. And what is it, anyway?" She is still pretending to sing, her eyes closed as if in rapture. "All this stuff about how we manage and heal the earth and so forth. It's a crock of shit!" She inhales and begins to sing again, staring at Proctor, who had begun to notice her lips were not moving quite the way they should.

"Shiiyiit," she yelps into the mass of building sound. "Nothing but . . . shiiyiit."

I don't know what to do with what she has summoned within me. It takes all my strength, all my resolve, to suppress it. But once the Thanks are over, we file out and rush away from the others, who are going to the Refectory, and sneak into one of the narrow corridors off the entryway to the Hall. We are already weak with the need to laugh, and once out of sight we both collapse into gales of laughter.

"They keep us in the dark and they feed us on shit," Laing manages to utter before choking with laughter again. "We are their mushrooms."

My face hurts. It is as if I have never truly laughed before, and indeed that may be the case.

When at last we regain our composure, Laing becomes accusing.

"There is something you are not telling me," she says. "I can tell you want to say it but you won't."

"If I told you, then you would . . . know," I say lamely. "I cannot tell anyone. It . . . is my burden alone. If I said anything to you, you would be punished along with me, wouldn't you? My burden would become your burden too."

Laing rolls her eyes and huffs at me. "You take yourself so seriously, Keller." She draws out the word *seriously* like she always does when she is teasing me: "seeeeeriously."

"You think the weight of the whole stupid world rests on your shoulders. Well, let me enlighten you. It doesn't. We don't matter, we never have, we never will. We think we're in charge of things. All that non-sense about our orchards, our borders, our farms. Us, us, *we Foundlanders,* as if we bring up the sun each day and put it down again at night. We are not the center of everything. You know as well as I do that we can be snuffed out like a candle." She snaps her fingers. "Just like that. Just like Dayna. We don't matter a damn. And I, for one, find that . . ." She searches for the word. It must be the first time she has put words to these thoughts, but her conviction is absolute. "It frees me," she declares at last. "I'm free because I know that I'm not important. Little me does not matter one whit."

As usual, there is something about her defiance that is thrilling and enviable. It is part of the force that draws us to her.

"Do you think you are a leader, Keller?" She narrows her eyes and doesn't miss a beat. "You may or may not be," she says. "Perhaps you are just a loner, and that is not always the same as a leader. You are more like me than you think. You think for yourself. That"—she raises her finger imperiously—"is why I decided I liked you."

She plucks at her shift. "And now I'm going to take this revolting garment off. Not that the other things they make us wear are much better. Come on. I can't wait for the beauty queen contest."

She has already gone a few paces when she whirls around, speaking in a voice that is so loud it almost seems she wants to be caught. "And I'll tell you something else. The Old People did better than we did. At everything! You can see it yourself! We have proof! Look at their wonderful things, the wonderful lives they had! Full of plenty and pleasure!"

"It wasn't plenty! It was waste! How many pairs of shoes did they need? You can't even walk in those things!"

Laing looks momentarily taken aback but I don't give her time to reply. The images are flying through my mind. All those breasts and buttocks on display . . . all that smiling. "They never *did* anything," I say quickly. I must outwit her. "They couldn't ride or shoot or look after themselves. They just lived in their soft palaces where—where it smelled sweet all the time, and nothing was heavy or difficult. I mean, what did they do all day long? Put on clothes?"

"That's right! And nothing *was* difficult. I *love* the shoes. They're fabulous!" She glares at me as if I have violated something sacred. "And if you weren't so high and mighty you would admit that you love the shoes too." She pauses to register her hit. And it is true—she has scored. She presses her advantage. "They were better at everything, better than we are. You've seen the objects. You *know* it's true."

I feel the pressure building in my chest, as if something I have been aching to say is about to find release. "I l-like the shoes." I falter because what I want to say sounds childish. I say it anyway. "But I only like it when we're . . . playing with them. It's the contest . . ." I can't go on under her withering stare, so I try to find something else to say and say it fiercely. "If they were so much better at everything, then why are they gone? Why did they fail? *Where are they?*"

"It wasn't their fault," blazes Laing. "Tribulation just came and annihilated them."

"It was their own fault," I blaze back.

"It wasn't."

"It was."

"How do you know?"

We face each other, panting and exhausted by our words. "This world is what we have," I say finally. "We only have each other against the trials of our time here on this earth. And everything we make and grow—we do it by ourselves. We make ourselves." I sound as if I am bleating, unable to persuade her in any way at all. And I'm not sure if I'm trying to convince her or myself. During the Sing and the Thanks and the partaking of the apples, I was somehow comforted by the presence of all who were gathered, by the swell of the song in the apple-scented air. I had given thanks with all my heart. "You're wrong," I say. "Just plain wrong. About everything."

"That's a load of bull. I'm right and you know it."

"Load of bull" is one of her new sayings. "Our lives are hard—and boring," she says. I can tell she wants to yell but dares not.

There is a tense silence between us as we bristle at each other again. We are both dealing in doubt and we are unsure of our footing. Are we having an argument? Arguments are forbidden.

Laing folds her arms. "I'll tell you something else," she declares. "There is no enemy. That's another crock of shit as well."

"How can you know that?" My mouth is so dry with fear I can hardly get the question out. Does she also know about the traitors meeting the men on the beach? "What have you seen?"

"That's just it—I've never seen the enemy. Not a single one, dead or alive. Have you ever seen one? Until they prove it to me, I'm not believing them any longer."

Over her shoulder I see Carrow coming back down the passageway, scuttering like a pale spider as she comes to make her claim on Laing.

"All this stuff about being a Tracker . . ." Laing trails off. As Carrow tries to link arms with her, she rolls her eyes, but only so that I can see. It is a huge relief. It can only mean that we are friends again.

Carrow has to pull away because all of the Committee Members appear, flanking Ms. Windsor. She is wearing her yellow glass eye mask, but now that we have seen so many images, it is no longer so unfamiliar. As they sweep by, we do as we always do: turn ourselves and our faces to the wall, even Laing.

LAING'S WORDS stay with me. Perhaps she is right. Perhaps all that we believe is set upon a crumbling, rotten foundation and the Time Before was much better. Maybe Tribulation just happened, like an accident, and was not deserved.

And I was less than honest. I couldn't be, not without endangering her. I never told Laing that she is right to be suspicious. The sacks the men gave Amos and her cohorts were not grain but tobacco. I have seen them tucked away behind the feed bins. I have even opened them and inhaled the rich, potent stench of it. The very smell of it is wrong in a way that makes my heart pound.

Does Amos know that I know? It is hard to tell. Despite the heat, she is as exacting as always, and I understand now what a brilliant instructor she is, how skilled and experienced and just plain useful.

I have begun to hate this feeling of confusion,

which is worse whenever I go to the hidden dwelling and am among the mass of things there. It is impossible to know why they had so many objects in their dwelling. I have begun to loathe the smell of the place too, a dead sweetness to it, rotting as it turns to mulch beneath its mantle of vegetation.

ONE EVENING, stinking of boiling bones from the slaughterhouse, I am returning long past suppertime back to the Refectory. I have been told to go to the Bath House and wash the smell off me, which is one of the good things about working in the slaughterhouse—it means an extra bath. I am hungry and feel sure that Parsons will have kept something aside for me.

The sky is such a lovely deep indigo color tonight and wisps of cloud drift across the moon. I'm so tired from working, but for some reason I feel happy. The track is a little muddy so I decide to take a shortcut down and across the grass, which, though wet, will at least keep my boots fairly clean. I do not relish the prospect of Ross or Bayles making me clean them before I am allowed to sleep. I have been surreptitiously watching Bayles to see what she is like when Laing is around, but she is too well trained to let too much show—only the odd lingering look followed by much loud bossing.

The slope runs down to the Nursery, which is mostly in darkness at this hour. I have forgotten so much of my time there, but I remember a few small things: the bibs we wore whenever we ate, the porridge drying stiff and brown in the bowls and how hard it was to wash off, the tasks, the sewing, the cleaning, the beginnings of our usefulness. I remember that my hands always hurt.

The coolness from the wet grass rises around me. I remove my boots, knot the laces, sling them around my neck, and just walk barefoot. When I look up, I notice a small circle of light that is also moving toward the Nursery, and now a face appears. I start because it is the very face I had been imagining only minutes before: Parsons, her big, kind face offering me the food that she has kept warm. Except now, her expression is as surprised as my own.

"Oh," she says, and then holds her hand to her chest as if to still a thudding heart. "It's you!" She snuffs out the light. "I—I—was wondering where you were." There is an awkward silence because she knows full well that I do not believe she was looking for me—I am hardly likely to get lost walking from the slaughterhouse to the Dwellings. She glances anxiously toward the Nursery and then looks back at me.

"I was going to the Refectory," I say. "I was hoping that maybe you had kept the supper warm for me. I'm starving!" I laugh, hoping to break the tension.

"Oh my . . ." She sounds regretful. "I was given a

free hour and so I . . ." She looks at me and her expression is almost sly. "Do you want to come with me?"

"Where?" Now I am really puzzled. What is she doing creeping about outside with a lamp at this hour?

"In there." She points to the Nursery that is only a few yards away. The Dormitory wing is in darkness although there is an orange square of lamplit window at the far end of the building, in the room where the Moms on night duty sit. "I have the key," she says, and takes a small iron key from her pocket. "To this door."

Without waiting for me to answer, she sets off toward the darkest end of the building.

"I can get you your supper after this," she says briskly. "It's just that I don't get this chance very often and if I don't do it now, I don't know when I will get another turn."

Turn at what? Mystified, I follow her to a door that is tucked into an alcove I hadn't noticed before. She turns the key and beckons me to enter first, then slips in herself. "Besides, they need it, some of us think. It might not be what others think, but it's our way. It does them good."

We are in a Dormitory, surrounded on all sides by small, sleeping forms bundled into the cribs. The air smells of sour milk, urine, and something else, a baby smell I cannot define other than it reminds me of baking bread. They sleep on their stomachs, their tiny limbs spread in a froglike position. There is something appallingly fragile about their skulls and the silken filaments of hair that only just cover the bone.

Without any further ado, Parsons picks one of them up, flipping her over and into her arms without the creature waking at all. She covers the tiny body with an equally tiny blanket, then sits herself down on the only chair in the room. She runs a finger over the girl-child's cheeks, then lifts her even closer and presses her own cheek to the girl-child's face. Her lips, close to the girl-child's ear, begin to move as she croons: "Lullaby and good night, thy mother's delight . . ." It is not the Sing at all, nothing like it for there are words to it. I have never heard any noise like it, but it is not unpleasant and the girl-child does not stir.

Parsons begins rocking back and forth in time to her own peculiar crooning and seems to have forgotten my presence altogether. "Lay thee down now and rest, may thy slumber be blessed. . . ."

I want her to hurry up and finish. What if a Mom comes in and catches us? The memory of my own trembling, upturned palms as they await the slice of the switch returns as if it had happened yesterday. But no Mom hears us or comes in to interrupt Parsons in her reverie. Her big red face is softened, suffused with something that I cannot quite name. Happiness? No, it is something else. For a moment or two, she meets my eye. Her expression does not change.

Another secret for a secret—all the meals kept warm for me, a spoon of honey, the cups of tea. She smiles, a faraway smile, and I smile back, but I don't think I can ever know the source of pleasure that gives rise to her particular smile. Another mystery. Rapture, that was what I wanted to call the look on her face.

"Pick one up," she whispers and presses her lips again to the sleeping child's head. "Go on."

But I remain rooted to the spot, unable to move at all. To take a girl-child up in my own arms? The thought terrifies me; I would not dare. Besides, I would not know how. And why? What does a sleeping girl-child know?

It's all secrets within secrets.

I'll keep your secret if you keep mine.

CHAPTER THIRTEEN

THE COMPETITION of beauty is begun.

"You should put this color on your eyes because they are blue. Blue goes with blue. That's what Laing says." Pike assists Ryan with the paint she is applying to her face. They are allotted five minutes in front of the mirror and they keep glancing anxiously at the hourglass I am holding.

I lean on the walls of the mirror room, uneasy at having to see myself in the mirror yet unable to turn away. Before Ryan and Pike are two images they have torn from the books, which they are using as a guide to show them how they must look. Once they realized it could be done, they all destroyed the books, ripping at the pages like wild animals.

"Hold still!" Ryan and Pike are engrossed in helping each other, which seems strange considering that in a short while they will be competing against each other to proclaim who among them is the most beautiful.

The smell of the paint, which is now scattered in its little pots and tubes all over the surface in front of the mirror, has a rancid, oily intensity to it that makes me regret accepting this timing task. The air in the dwelling seems alive tonight, crackling with our nerves and energy. Bayles has let us past, all of us, while she pretended to be asleep. Is Laing paying her in some way for this?

I push the thought away and tell Ryan and Pike that their turn is up. They are desperate, begging for a moment longer. Like many of the others, they have put the red paint on their mouths, pasted their cheeks deathly white, and painted dark lines on the rims of their eyes. Their faces resemble skulls with big, hollow eyes and grotesque, fleshy lips, as if their mouths had never decomposed.

They troop out and the next two push past them, fighting for space at the mirror. Outside there is shrieking and high-pitched chatter that is deceiving, for there is a ferocity to their excitement. The room is packed—the whole Patrol has left the dormitory. A wild and stupid risk but we are crazed with our idea.

Piles of clothing that we have found in the closets are heaped everywhere, and all the other Novices have their arms and hands thrusting out of sleeves, tugging and fastening buttons. Walsh has found a bottle of sickly-smelling liquid that, when she pushes down on the top part, squirts out in a fine spray. Its smell lies in a layer over the other layers of smells: our nervous sweat, the fatty smell of the candles, the face paint, and the sweet, musty odor of the house. It overpowers me. The feeling I often have in this place—the urge to run—takes over for a second or two, but I promised Laing I would stay, if not take part. *It won't be right if you're not there,* she had said.

Shoes are flung everywhere around the room, and it is clear that they all plan to wear them despite the fact that none of us can walk in them. Laing claps her hands, commanding silence. She gets up on Dayna's bed, which has become her usual pulpit. She has ignored me for days because she is so mad at my refusal to take part, even though she has guessed the real reason. The fact that she has not said anything to me must be out of pity. She must know that I am ugly—too ugly to even pretend I could take part in this competition.

"Now remember, when I say so, we are all to close our eyes," Laing says. "That gives you a chance to work your 'look.' Then you go to the end of the passageway and shout 'Ready!' And remember that you must each call out your own name. Your *new* name," she adds severely. "Has everyone chosen their name? When it's your turn, you call out your new name. Then everyone can open their eyes because they know that you are ready. You will begin to walk down the passageway and come in here. You will stand on the bed while we all look at you and then you must wait while we all raise our hands. The more hands that show for you, the higher you are in the competition and the more beautiful you are. And remember, you mustn't walk too fast. In the images they walk like this." She thrusts her hips forward. "It must have helped them to lean back when they wore their shoes," she says. "Now, I am going to get ready and then everyone has to be all set to start."

She leaps off the bed, her hair flying and the shadows of her graceful limbs pinned for a moment on the facing wall. Then she takes up a bundle, the actual clothes concealed in a shawl, and disappears into the mirror room.

There follows a short pause where we all silently acknowledge that there is no doubt about the outcome of this competition, and then the hubbub begins anew. They are all in a partial state of undress because nobody wants to put on their whole outfit, having realized the importance of the element of surprise. Our military training has not been totally wasted, it seems.

The door of the mirror room bangs open and Laing reappears, wrapped from head to foot in a black sheet. Only her face is visible, and hardly that—just enough to see her eyes, huge and round, peering from the swaths. We stare at her, taking some time to realize that she is in some form of disguise. Ignoring our surprise, she tells everyone to get into their viewing positions.

"Begin!" she cries, and at last there is a real silence, one of total concentration. "Walsh goes first! Everyone, close your eyes!"

Because I am not taking part, I keep mine open. But the others are as obedient as they would be if they were at a Silent Beating or a Sing. Walsh hurtles down to the end of the passageway with her bundle of clothes.

She goes into one of the side rooms, then reemerges in her finery: a long white garment pulled in at the waist with a thick black belt. She has on black boots and a tight woolen hat, and around her throat is the oddest scarf I have ever seen, made out of some kind of bird feathers. She wears some of the metal chains and her lips are smeared gold-brown. She is gripping the long handle of a kind of rectangular bag on little wheels, which she drags behind her as she commences her walk down the passageway. It is astounding because she does seem to be balancing on the heel spikes of the boots, although she has to be walking on tiptoe.

"You forgot to say your name." Laing pops out

from the shadows, a bad-tempered crone shuffling in her sheet down the passageway. "Go back," she says bossily.

Walsh turns around and begins again. "Tiffany," she shrieks. We crowd the doorway, stepping aside to let her into Dayna's Room. The bag on wheels squeaks along behind her and she abandons it as she steps onto the bed. Our eyes rake her, taking in every detail as though we are learning something we need to know.

"How many choose Tiffany?" Laing's voice comes out as a muffled yell through her sheet. At first no one makes a move, and Laing is forced to repeat her question. "Come on! You have to choose. How many for Tiffany?"

Begrudgingly she raises her own hand, more to start off the others than anything. Still, Walsh is pleased. Sweat trickles down from under her woolen hat and over her face paint, which is already starting to smear. A few more hands are raised.

"Keller, you have to keep count," says Laing. She is getting tired of running things; she wants to enjoy herself. "Okay. Get off the bed now. Next! Bella! Ashley! Hurry up!"

And so it goes, one nervous Patrol member after another, with her clothes so agonized over, her churning stomach, her anxiety to be beautiful before our merciless gaze. And yet how badly each wants to be looked at. Some have squeezed into pants so tight that the outlines of their very genitals are visible, while others seem to glide down the passageway in long, brilliantly colored garments. Their faces, caked in the paint, are lost and have become something else. They frequently fall over in the impossible shoes. They try to smile. Pike has on a pair of the dark eyeglasses, although one of the pieces of glass is cracked. A Novice called Roberts has found a bizarre cup shaped out of paper, which she carries as if there were some hot liquid inside, and it is true, many of the people in the images carry these paper cups. Another carries one of those slim silver boxes held close to her ear.

We watch one another like prey, a special watchfulness descending as each one springs onto the bed to submit herself to our scrutiny and our judgment. No one escapes unless they are cowards like me. And I am the only coward, safe and hidden behind my contempt and my disdain. This competition is not an exercise in enjoyment but as grueling a test as any we have endured on the training field.

I cannot bear each conclusion where I have to count the hands, the shrugs from the crestfallen ones who have received only a few hands and the elation of those who get many.

"Candy!" shrieks Laing, and Carrow appears.

She wears a long red garment that hangs gracefully from her bony frame and falls straight to the floor. She is barefoot and, apart from a broad, bronze cuff on her thin arm, she wears no other adornment. She has darkened her pale eyelashes and her lips are a bright, startling red. She has cut her hair even shorter and there is something quite scarily beautiful about the way the paint has changed and defined her face. To my shock, I realize that I truly think she looks beautiful. In fact, it is obvious to me that she is the most beautiful. Her restraint in choosing her clothes, the single red garment that drapes her body, lends her a loveliness I have never seen before. In that strangeness of her, bordering on deviancy, there is another kind of beauty I had never thought possible.

But my approval is not the approval she seeks. She hates me. I have stolen her friend. Her eyes burning, she searches for the only hand she wants to see raised. Laing appraises her coolly but her hand remains by her side. Filled with an unexpected pity, I add my own illegal hand to the two others who have cautiously raised theirs. Laing turns to look at the three of us who have chosen Carrow. She's still covered in the sheet so it is impossible to see her expression, but something about the way she is holding herself lets me know that she is not at all pleased. I don't care. I keep my hand in the air but the other two take their hands down. Carrow fires a look of pure hatred at me. Her whole long, sinuous body quivers with fury and humiliation. As she bounds off the bed she looks as though she is going to kill me. She wrenches off the garment and stands there with it, panting, her skin translucent over her heaving rib cage. Then, half-naked but without looking back, she flies down the passageway, the garment trailing in her hand like a flame.

The silence that follows is broken by a single terrible sob as Carrow heads toward the kitchen and the hidden opening that leads up and out to the forest. When the door opens, we can hear rain and a rumble of thunder. We shuffle guiltily for a moment or two. Then the door slams shut.

"Right, that's one hand for Candy," says Laing. And then she glares at me. "I thought you said you didn't want to take part," she hisses.

I cannot take any more. I also want to leave this place but there is something even more powerful holding me here. Laing is preparing to make her entrance. She is on her way down to the end of the passageway, still wrapped in her winding sheet, when she vanishes into the side room and lets the tension mount. A few minutes pass and then she makes her appearance. A collective gasp, a noise like a wave crashing, and then someone lets out a whoop. And then they are all howling like a pack of she-wolves. Laing grins and continues down the passageway dressed in a raincoat made of some transparent stuff. And beneath the raincoat, the surprise she has hoarded all this time: gold undergarments, the likes of which are wholly indecent, wholly fascinating. One shimmering piece covers her breasts, and one piece has been shaped to cover her genitals. The muscles of her stomach and thighs ripple as she strides toward us. She wears a huge, floppy white hat that shades her face, although each time she moves her head her painted eyes flash from beneath the brim. Her shoes are also white, built upon platforms, and they have leathern laces crisscrossed up her strong calves, right up to the knees. She pulls off the hat and tosses her hair, mounting the bed in one single triumphant step. Then she wheels her arm in the air and flings the hat high.

Their howling turns to shrieking. They cling to one another and collapse in cackling heaps on the bed, delirious, as if they were all in the grip of some crazy, unending fever. "You won!" They are screaming at her. "You are the winner!" Her arms are extended and she is tramping up and down on the soft bed wiggling her hips, her head thrown back, her eyes closed in laughter.

The Beauty Queen.

And this is what I remember now: a kind of crazy, shared bliss. I remember her as she danced on the bed in her warrior shoes and the shining gold cloth that barely covered her breasts or her loins. But I could take no more. Amid all the commotion, no one noticed when I crept out of the hidden opening and into the pouring rain. Released at last, relief surging through me, I ran through the dark and the wet until they stepped out from the dripping trees.

"There is no time," they said. "Get back to the Dwellings as fast as you can if you are to be saved."

I smelled the cigarette smoke on their skin.

I felt the rough hands of Smith as she clasped my face and held it close to her own.

"Run," she hissed.

Then Amos shoved me. "Go, you stupid Novice! They are on their way. We did not have time to save you." And her voice cracked. "We tried . . . but they were ahead of us all the way."

I turned, shaking and ready to flee as they had told me, but Amos gripped me. "When they ask you, you must deny it all. You were never involved. You never knew."

Rain streaked the bone and leathern skin of her face. She must have seen my face too, the doubt and the fear. "It is not treason, Keller," she said. "It is survival."

CHAPTER FOURTEEN

When they lead them to the Circle, there are still traces of the face paint smudged upon their faces. Their hair is stringy, uncombed, and they shiver because they are not fully clothed. Some are still wearing tatters of the forbidden clothing, but for the most part, it must have been ripped from their bodies. They have been tied together with lengths of rope, like fillies being brought from an outlying farm to be broken in.

In the dawn we await them in the Cleansing Circle, dressed in our white shifts, our hair pulled away from our scrubbed faces, our bodies also scrubbed clean so that we may be pure and clear in our thoughts. The miscreants are led around the inside of our Circle so that we may touch them and begin to heal them for the greater good of the earth and the Foundlanders. Our hands flutter over their naked skin and they flinch from us. Parsons's eyes shine with tears and her hands pass over the ones she can reach, pressing upon theirs until the Prefects pull them away.

"We are pure and you have soiled us," we chant over and over, so that all anyone can hear is the whispers of our shame. "You must be cleansed."

We must rid them of their filth, the contamination they have brought with them because of their forbidden involvement with the objects from the Time Before: the greasy face paint; the clothing that, out here in the fresh air, looks faded and rancid with age and mold.

The Prefects come with their buckets of scalding water and bars of hard, carbolic soap. They untie the ropes and strip the remaining rags from the Novices' bodies and begin to scrub the soap into lather with stiff brushes. They take the brushes and begin with a grim vigor that makes some of the Novices cry out as they extend their reddening limbs.

The soapy water slides off their tainted skin, washing their misdeeds away, soap and water offering the chance of renewal. Now we may all begin afresh and reconnect to our mission to cleanse and heal the earth after its desecration by the Old People. The strong, clean smell of the soap rises and the Novices now stand before us, their bodies raw and naked and shivering. The last of the rinsing water streams over their upturned faces and slicks their hair to their heads.

"We are cleansed," they murmur and raise their arms to the sky. "We shall atone. We shall be worthy."

The Prefects tie them back up and lead them away to the Darkness, where they will remain until it is deemed they have reclaimed their purity.

Neither Carrow nor Laing was with them. They have disappeared.

I slipped into the Dormitory, knowing that soon I would be summoned. I lay on my bed and shook with cold fear. All I could hear was Amos, over and over, her breath sawing through her lungs: *It is not treason . . . it is survival.*

I had returned, panting and shaking, and still smelling of the perfume and the face paint. I took some water from a bucket in the kitchen and scrubbed myself. Parsons saw me and said nothing, but I could tell she knew something terrible was happening. I went to the Dormitory and just sat on my bed. When the Prefects marched in to get me, I knew then that the others had been found. They were all puffed up with the importance they feel whenever there is to be some kind of ceremony or punishment. They could barely contain themselves and, once they had told me to change and get into my shift for the Cleansing Circle, they began to whisper among themselves. They kept turning and eyeing me with great and excited suspicion.

They will never believe me if I tell them I know

nothing of this disobedience, but they will if I tell them I took no part in the competition of beauty. They all know, and would accept, that I am too ugly and too serious to have ever had the guts to involve myself in such a folly. Behind my back they will no doubt snigger about it, about my cowardice, about the big, plain, watchful loner.

I should confess. I must suffer with my Patrol.

But what actually happens is worse.

THE DAYS that follow are empty of all meaning. No one will allow me to confess. Each time I try to send for Gosse in order to tell her that I too deserve to be punished, they will not do it. I even ask for an audience with the Headmistress but it is denied me.

I eat very little, sleep fitfully, and endure the tasks that are set for me. I am shunned by all, but in my distracted state it is of little consequence to me. I wait to be summoned, and on the third day it is Gosse, stumping into the Armory, who comes to tell me that Ms. Windsor awaits my presence.

Gosse walks with me across the Quadrangle, too close, as is her habit. We walk up the stairs and she stations herself against the wall in the passageway, just a little way from the door that leads to Ms. Windsor's quarters. I continue past her and knock on the door. A Housekeeper opens it and ushers me in.

In the daytime the rooms Ms. Windsor occupies are filled with a flat light that comes in from the narrow windows facing north. She is seated at her desk and does not look up when I come in, concentrating instead upon her writing. She uses one of the quills, pausing to dip it once into the inkstand before she acknowledges me by gesturing with it, indicating that I am to sit on the fragile chair that has been placed opposite the desk. The nib of the quill scratches on the parchment, the only sound for some time. The unliving plant is still in place, as are the grinning orange timepiece on its little legs and the long chair.

Despite the sunlight outside, the high ceilings ensure that these rooms remain chilly. I check to see if the fur that keeps her warm is still thrown across her bed, but the doors to that room are closed. I can hear the Housekeeper sweeping the floors within. I look back to the desk, suddenly aware that as I am observing, I am also being observed. She has stopped writing and her hand lies motionless upon the jeweled box that contains the white powder, as if the sensation of it under her palm is, for the time being, sufficient to quell the need to open it and take the powder into her mouth. There is an air of jubilation about her.

"I suppose you were amazed at how long it took us to find you out," she says, almost indulgently. "I admit we were slow . . . the heat, and other difficulties . . . but we had our suspicions."

She draws breath to say something else, then stops as another Housekeeper bustles in with a tray laden with a teapot, cups, and a small pitcher. She lays the tray upon the desk. As she turns away, the Housekeeper gives me a long look. Ms. Windsor conveys her impatience with a short expulsion of breath, obviously wanting her gone. The Housekeeper scurries out.

I study the tea tray. Sweat prickles all over my body. She will always outwit me—she has not even given me a chance to deny anything at all. She knows I was there, part of the whole thing.

The teapot, a precious thing from the Time Before, is made of the most exquisite, fine clay and is glazed in blue and white. There are images upon it—funny little dwellings with curved roofs, doves, wooden footbridges, and trees with long, trailing branches. The spout of the teapot is chipped. I want to step into the peaceful blue and white world of it, away from these frightening games and codes and rules, cross over the bridges and lie down under the delicate branches of those trees and listen to the water running over the stones in the little stream. Why am I destined for this colorless, sequestered, and stern world that is ours, that is mine?

Ms. Windsor pours the tea into only one cup but she doesn't drink. The steam rises from the cup as she glances down at the parchment on the desk before her, smoothing it flat with her hand.

"The Novices in your Patrol have begun the process of being cleansed," she says. "They have been purified in the Cleansing Circle and after the allotted time in the Darkness, some, not all, will return and reclaim their full purity. Then they can rejoin us, renewed and ready to pull their weight once again."

What does she mean, "some"? Who will not be returned? She must mean Laing and Carrow. Are they together? And even then, in all this misery, I feel that now-familiar jolt of jealousy.

Ms. Windsor picks up the teapot to pour a cup for me.

She looks at me then, her eyes again with that jubilant, hectic glitter. Her skin is dry and tight and I have a sudden vision of the skull beneath. For an instant something like a spasm of pain seems to clutch at her. She looks tired and there is a weeping sore in the corner of her mouth. When she reaches for the little jeweled box, the birdlike bones of her hand shift beneath her papery skin.

"My belief is that, for a short time, you fell under the spell of Laing. You acted against your better judgment. We all have such lapses. But then when you refused to take part in that repugnant costume parade, you came to your senses. You held it in contempt. At least this is my assumption. And that was the right thing to do. I believe too that when you went to that place alone, during your walkabout, you were trying to signal to us its location. You were trying to signal many things, I believe. I should have picked up on these signs much earlier than I did. Do you have anything more to add to your account of that walkabout?" Her voice softens. "Why did you not just come to me directly? You must have known I would listen to you."

"I have nothing to add."

For a moment she looks almost crestfallen. "Yes, well, this practice of the walkabout is to be discontinued." That is all she says for some time. A silence stretches between us. Then she spreads her hands and proclaims in the high, brittle voice she uses when she addresses our assembled community, "The growing cycle is almost complete and soon we shall be ready for a harvest. We have managed a whole cycle! We are redeemed!"

The tea in my cup has become tepid. I put it down on the table. "We are redeemed," I answer tonelessly. I have betrayed my whole Patrol by not sticking with them; I ran away. I do not know what to say.

"Stop sulking. Please. You see, you are coming with me, Keller. This parchment here, which I have now written out and signed, relieves you of your duties as a Novice and as a Tracker. You are to become my assistant. I have selected you."

She stands up and goes to look out the window. A few voices drift up as a group of Seamstresses with their baskets crosses the Quadrangle. I wonder what they thought of the clothes ripped from the bodies of the Novices during the Cleansing Circle. Their days are spent wrestling with greasy wool and bolts of linen that are stacked like thick gray pillars in their workshop. What would they have made of the ragged rainbow softness of the found clothes?

"Yes, we are going to Johns. It is there that I shall train you in matters of holding our community together, in sustaining our purpose here in this land." She pauses and then repeats, "I have selected you."

"Why?"

She smiles one of her tight little smiles again. "Because I think you want it. You have great capability. You think, you observe, you see many sides to a question, but in the end, loyalty drives you more than anything. And great loyalty is what lies behind the ability to be ruthless."

I close my eyes. I feel winded and fight for breath.

"And, Keller, though you may not know it, you *are* ruthless. Why do you think Amos chooses you to shoot the useless animals? She has seen, as I have, that you can make difficult decisions and then carry them out. I can draw out this quality in you." Her tone is full of something that sounds like excitement. "I can mold you in my image! You are a believer, not a doubter. And you are true to our cause. You will never let yourself succumb to the enemy. The thought of yielding to them disgusts you, does it not? It is not in your nature."

"I was too ugly to take part in the competition of beauty," I mutter, but she is so caught up in her enthusiasm that she ignores me.

"Tell me again," she says. Spots of color appear upon her cheeks and her hand twitches for the jeweled box. "Did you see the snake? It is here, I know it. I'm sure of it."

"I don't know," I croak. "It was dark. It disappeared into the dark."

"But you resisted it, did you not?" She opens the box and loads a tiny heap of the powder onto her fingertip. "You see, you did not succumb to its power. When you become my acolyte, I shall guide you in everything. You shall have no other confusing voices to listen to—only me. You will live with me, breathe the air I breathe, and you will serve me so that you may learn all I can impart to you. You need not be subject to any other influence so that your learning is unimpeded by the opinions and thoughts of others."

"Where is Laing?" I am terrified by this vision of becoming hers and hers alone.

"Ah," she says. "Laing." She pauses awhile. Her

finger moves to touch the sore on her mouth, then she sits down in her chair again, her skirt rustling as she arranges it around her. She seems calmer now. "Laing is defiled beyond redemption, I think you'll agree. I think we'll just impregnate her and have done with it. When we catch her, that is. And I have word that the Trackers are closing in."

She folds her hands, the left again gripping the right so that it might not rise to the little box of powder too soon. "She may have other uses. I don't know yet. What do you think we should do with Laing?"

She waits, her head cocked to one side inquiringly. "You see, that is what power gives you. You can make that choice. You can decide." She picks up the teapot. "When you come with me to Johns, if you serve me well as my assistant, then one day you would be in a position to decide her fate. In fact, you may decide the fate of almost anyone." She starts to refill her cup with tea, pouring it in a clear red-gold stream that curls into the teacup with the blue pattern of little curved bridges and bowed trees that bend to pools of water.

"No," I whisper. "Not impregnation."

She puts her cup down with an annoyed little clink. "I don't understand all this fuss about impregnation. If you are fertile, then it is your duty and that is that." She frowns. "There is, however, another choice."

"What choice is that?" The scent of the tea mingles with the scent of crushed geraniums.

"I could have her given away."

"Given? To whom?" There is a sense of falling, of being pulled into some void of disbelief.

"You see, on occasion we must purge ourselves of a ruined Novice. People beyond our borders want us because we are so perfect. To us a ruined Novice may be soiled, but to them a ruined Novice is of great value. Their standards are so much lower. Of course it is something we do only under extreme duress and with extreme reluctance. But we do as we must. We cannot under any circumstance be defiled by one of our own. I think you would agree."

She considers me a while longer, weighing whether or not to continue. In the end, she does. "It has become necessary for another reason. Sometimes I must give away a Novice in return for my powder. I am in permanent pain, you see. Indeed, I am in agony. And there are those beyond our borders with whom I would never ordinarily have any dealings, but who have supplies of this painkilling powder. The Committee Members agree that I cannot lead if I am in terrible pain, and so it was concluded that this was the correct thing to do. These men beyond our borders especially savor the Novices, I have learned. Even though to us those Novices have failed, to the disgusting mutants beyond, they are still tall, pure, and lovely. Of course, I never give a pure one, only one who is beyond redemption. I could not live with my conscience otherwise."

"Laing is my friend," I say, and my voice breaks. "My best friend." I am sinking now under the weight of what she has just told me.

It is as if I have slapped her. Color rises in her cheeks and she stands up suddenly, pushing her chair so that it scrapes on the floor.

"Friend!" Tiny flecks of spittle settle on her lips and I avert my eyes from her. "Yes, I fancy you thought she was your friend, but she has betrayed you on every score. You wait until we catch her and she will crack open like an egg! If she were loyal to you, she would be with you. But she is with Carrow."

I cry out, "No! They must have fled separately."

"Well, they are together now, at least this is what the Trackers report."

She leans forward and to my shock puts her hand on my arm. Her touch makes my skin crawl, as though she carries some magical charge.

"You know as well as I do that friends are nothing but a dangerous distraction from our purpose here. You have seen firsthand what can happen when you fall into what you think of as friendship." Her fingers, at first light on my arm, now grip it. "No, Keller. You are no longer to think of friends. You are to think instead of *allies*. Leaders cultivate allegiance, not this disruptive thing you, in your youthfulness, think of as friendship. There are no such things as friends."

She takes her hand from my arm. "That is how a leader thinks."

There is a knock on the door. Ms. Windsor turns her head and then grips the edge of the desk, as if she has suddenly felt a stab of pain.

The Housekeeper bustles in, full of the importance of one bearing dramatic news. She glances at me and then whispers something to Ms. Windsor, shielding her mouth with her hand so that I cannot hear what is said. When she is done, she stands back, even more swelled with importance now that her tale is told.

Ms. Windsor turns, sweeping her skirts around her, and snatches the yellow eye mask that had been lying on her desk and puts it on. Without any more preparation, she makes for the door. Halfway across the room she suddenly wheels around and, with a biting impatience, says, "Come on. Come with me."

The Housekeeper follows us out. I can feel her eyes on my back all the way down the passage.

CHAPTER FIFTEEN

CARROW IS WEARING her long red garment. She must have put it back on after she left. The face that had formerly been contorted in anger and humiliation is now vacant, a kind of peace to it that only absence can bring. Two of the stones she has used to weight herself are still strapped to her limbs, but she has washed up into a pool beneath a tree. One of the ropes attached to the rocks has snagged on a tree root. Her body is not yet bloated or distorted by the horror of her death.

A pair of ringed turtledoves coos in the trees overhead and the sun is warm on our backs. The banks of the river are perfumed with late white dog roses growing upon their sides, and the water is lit with the secret green tree-light from the branches overhead. Some of the rose blossoms float serenely upon the green water. Pulled by the slight current, the wet garment billows gently over her thin body. Her pale face has been washed free of the paint, and in death she is an even stranger beauty.

For an instant I see her in hot tears, flying down the passageway of the forbidden dwelling, the door slamming. Where did she go? What did I know of her longings, her needs, her hopes? *Laing,* I say inwardly, *Laing. Look at what we have done.*

Two Trackers have found her. They are standing on the banks awaiting the arrival of our party: me, Ms. Windsor, and the Headmistress. Their hobbled horses graze in a small patch of meadow just beyond the banks. I wonder why they have not dragged her from the river. Did the sad loveliness of the scene prevent them?

"We tracked her for some time, and then we lost her. To the north, another Tracker has got the other one. They'll bring her in presently," says one of the Trackers. "This one must have committed this deed only hours ago."

It is true. Carrow's body is not decomposed. She must have hidden away with some brilliance for she had only that bright red garment to cover her nakedness. I have underestimated her from the beginning, and now it is too late.

Ms. Windsor quivers with anger. "Get her out," she says. "And take that dress off her."

The Trackers clamber down the banks, wade into

the pool, and start dragging her out. The Headmistress sighs, and I have the sense that this is not the first time she has witnessed such a scene. Others must have plunged into this despair. There are no longer any first times for the Headmistress, not for anything. She has not spoken to me. It is as if I am already lost to her. I am seized with an urge to talk to her, to reach out, even to take her hand.

The Trackers hold Carrow between them, one carrying her shoulders and the other supporting her legs. They walk sideways up the bank, the body swaying, and then they dump her on the level ground at the top. They peel the wet dress off her. A shaft of light falls through the trees upon her wet skin. Ms. Windsor must notice the filtering light and commands them to move the body to another, darker place and to wrap it head to foot in a horse blanket. This they do, taking ropes from their saddlebags and lashing the body into its shroud. They work efficiently, with hardly a word, as is our way.

Ms. Windsor is coming toward me, fury twisting her features into a snarl. Her hair, normally pulled tight to her skull, has come loose around her face. For the first time I notice fine white hair at her temples. Her cloak flies out behind her as she moves.

"This," she says, pointing a shaking finger at Carrow's corpse. "This!" For the first time she seems to be so angry she cannot speak. She pauses and recovers a degree of composure. Even through the yellow eye mask I can see how bright her eyes are. "This was what the enemy would like to see. This is how they would like to see us. If they could see this, they would win. They would rejoice in this very sight. This—this—passive creature floating—floating—uselessly in the water! That Novice has succumbed to the most insidious of inner voices . . . and . . ." She almost stamps her foot in rage. "Weak! She was weak!" Her voice pierces the beauty of the green glade. "Take her away. Bury her in an unmarked grave and tell no one." As if they might violate her order, her voice rises even higher and she all but screams after them: "Not a living soul!"

The Trackers go and get their horses. They load up the body, now so tightly bound in a rough blanket that I cannot even say which end is her head or her feet. Their faces are grimly respectful of Ms. Windsor, but there are several inquiring glances my way. They mount up and, without further ado, move their horses and their burden into the depths of the forest.

The Headmistress watches them as they move off and then looks back to the river and its lovely green pool, which just moments ago held the body of one of her Novices. The turtledoves call again and motes of dust dance in the slanting sunlight.

"It is peaceful here," she says. She picks up the red garment that has been cast on the forest floor. She runs the fabric through her fingers for a moment or two, then she walks down the bank to the edge of the pool and lays it back into the water. It swirls away with the gentle current before slipping downstream.

Ms. Windsor makes no attempt to intervene. She presses her lips together into a thin white line as the garment disappears from view. Showing her age for the first time I can ever remember, the Headmistress climbs stiffly back up the bank. She seems cloaked in sadness. She pauses and looks at me, a long, hard look that sears me to the very core. And she walks straight past Ms. Windsor without another word.

GOSSE GUARDS ME night and day, and I am in effect a prisoner. I am put to work helping with the harvest. Since finding Carrow's body, I have had no further audience with Ms. Windsor. She has been constantly at the site of the hidden dwelling; no preparations have been made for her, or I suppose I should say *our*, departure.

The Prefects are exempted from the harvest, because they have another harvest: They are raiding the hidden dwelling, emptying it of its contents, lumbering down the ridge and along the river with all the found objects from the house.

They have unlocked the high gates around the places where they keep the stores of found objects and they carry the new finds into the long buildings, where they decontaminate them, or so they say. When I am walking up from the fields with Gosse limping along beside me, I sometimes see an object I recognize: the lilac bed covering from Dayna's bed, the long gray window panel that served no purpose as a window, and the two-wheeled object that I tried to describe to Smith. The Prefects wear overalls and headgear to protect them from the toxic objects—something that in all our nights of discovery had never even occurred to us, as if everything we had ever been taught just evaporated in our obsession with the place. Perhaps we are all doomed to die from the poison secreted in the fibers and smooth surfaces of all those things from the Time Before, especially me, the guarded favorite, because I was not cleansed.

For some reason, the thought does not worry me. I have begun to wonder about the truth of many things. If found objects were so toxic, why do we have so many of them in daily use?

THE TRACKERS bring Laing within days.

"They caught her easily. She has been put in the Darkness." Gosse is quick to tell me how Laing let herself be caught, how she surrendered without a fight.

"Will she be cleansed?"

"The Novices in your Patrol who partook of the Cleansing Circle will return," says Gosse. "But Laing will not. For her and her alone, the drums will beat tomorrow."

My heart seems to flutter and then fold, as though collapsing in upon itself.

The drums. I cannot bear the drums.

They begin in the very early morning, that colorless, nameless hour that is neither dark nor dawn. The rhythm is slow and frightening, increasing in tempo as the sun rises. We are ordered out of the Dwellings and made to gather near the mound just outside the gateway to the Quadrangle. From this point you can see the farmland spreads all around. Already the weather is turning and we must finish the harvest soon.

The drummers, a Prefect and a Tracker whom I do not recognize, appear through a low-lying mist that threads its way across the fields. The drums are slung across their bodies and their faces are expressionless as they each take up a position on either side of the gateway. Why does the sound of the drums make me so scared? I cannot bear the relentless sound. The pain above my left eye begins again, like a physical echo of the insistent sound that now reverberates off the stone walls of the College buildings.

I look around and everyone is shivering. We clutch at ourselves, wrapping our arms around our own bodies, forbidden as it is to comfort one another with any kind of touch or embrace. Some of the girl-children are still sleepy and bewildered, as they stare at the drummers and the growing crowd of women called by the drum, trooping out of all the buildings and coming over the fields from the farms.

In the distance, I can make out Smith and all her apprentices, grim-faced, striding along the wide path that leads from her workshop to our buildings. And Amos has also arrived. She hardly acknowledges me—that is her normal way—but she is even more remote than usual. How badly I need some sign from her, yet what could she tell me?

The crowd moves forward and I try to maneuver myself away from Gosse and closer to Amos. I must send her a signal, some sign that I need to speak with her or Smith. But when I am close enough to whisper to her, she mutters at me to move away, to get back to my position, almost as if she is frightened to be seen so close. Loneliness overwhelms me.

The mist is lifting now. I look out over the fields and ridges, lined with gleaming light from the rising sun, the ocean beyond . . . and beyond that, all that I do not know. I want everything. I am a glutton of some kind—greedy for what? Life? Power? Friendship? A fur coat? I want, I want . . . there is no end to my desires.

The sun burns off the mist, the drumbeats build . . . and then they come.

First come the Committee Members together with the Headmistress. Behind them two Prefects lead

Laing, pulling her up whenever she stumbles, which is often. A suppressed gasp, like a kind of sigh, rises from the crowd. Laing is deathly pale and emaciated. They have kept her clothed as she was the day she was caught. The golden garments are shredded and soiled and the transparent raincoat is missing a sleeve. The warrior shoes, with their laced-up leggings, have cut into her legs, which are running with sores. Her matted hair covers her face except for the brief moments when she tries to push it away so that she can see her way.

She is led to the crest of the mound, where the chair has been placed and a third Prefect awaits with the shears. Behind that Prefect, farther down the mound, is Bayles, holding a sack for the clippings. She bites her lip and closes her eyes behind her thick eyeglasses, then turns her face away.

The Prefects push Laing down onto the chair, although they need use no force. She merely drops. When they pull her head back, there is no protest. Her throat is whitely exposed, as if they are to slit it. The drumbeats increase and the Prefects begin hacking at her hair. The sun has risen now. The drums stop and the silence they leave is worse. A dog barks somewhere in the distance. Laing's hair falls away in clumps and Bayles walks up the mound, taking it up in handfuls and placing it in the sack in which it is to be burned.

When the shearing is done, Laing is made to stand

up, which again she does meekly, almost jumping up, obedient and obliging although her face is blank, as if she is not really among us at all. Her scalp is bare, studded with tufts of hair and bleeding in places where they have cut her. A single trickle of blood runs down over her forehead and around one of her empty eyes, but she does not appear to notice it. She is looking at me, I am sure, right at me, and I cannot help myself—a tiny cry escapes my lips. But there is no response in her gaze. She is not there.

They lead her back down the mound and she is made to kneel before Ms. Windsor. Ms. Windsor touches her shoulder with one small hand. Laing is forced to get up again. The Prefects pull her forward. She stumbles after them in her stolen shoes and her forbidden golden garments. I don't know where they are taking her.

The rest of the Patrol is led out of the Darkness.

They have a horrible, fumbling newness to them, as if they have just been born and have yet to acquire the skin that will protect them. They stand for a while before us, then they are led away to the Seamstresses to be clothed anew. Over the following days, now that we have forgiven them, they are given extra food and made to do only light duties in the kitchens and vegetable gardens until they are able to take up their former training. They are meek and grateful for these concessions.

In the line at the Refectory, the only time I can get near any of them, I try to speak to them. They do not avoid me, but they are distant and polite with me. They even seem a little afraid of me. I am a reminder of something terrible they once did but can no longer quite name. No mention is made of the forbidden dwelling, the clothes, Dayna's Room. If I try to talk to them, they tell me in a dazed monotone that they have been cleansed, emerged from the mire as new. They seem to hardly know who I am. Gradually, as they regain their strength, they return to their Tracker training, thrusting their bayonets into sacks of straw, galloping bareback, mounting and dismounting at a pace, and stripping and cleaning their weapons with all the dedication expected of them.

I am not allowed to join them. I am now both outcast and chosen. I am no longer given any horses to ride. I am given my duties in the slaughterhouse and spend many hours in the fields. Gosse follows me around like some sort of mournful guard dog. I am no longer allowed to do any of the things I used to do. I cannot even read the pages in the Library anymore. It is as if no one knows what to do with me pending Ms. Windsor's orders, and she is thoroughly occupied with the treasure of found objects and what has become the search for the rest of it within the Gated Community.

Gosse has told me more about the Gated Community. Long sought after, never found, it is not just one forbidden dwelling, but a whole host of them, collapsed and sunk under vegetation, full of rats and all ruins for the most part. Parsons also whispers to me, and I overhear the Prefects as they talk outside the Dormitory doors when on duty. The Librarians whisper, the Seamstresses and the Nurses whisper. An enormous bounty of objects, more than has ever been found in our lifetime, a toxic treasure trove. Found by us, by Laing.

That night I lie in my narrow little bed and conjure her image, the sores on her legs, her bleeding scalp, her dulled eyes. The rest of the Patrol seems to be asleep. Inspection has come and gone without a murmur. It is colder tonight, a hint of frost perhaps. No one whispers now after lights-out; there is no skittering out through the night, no cloying face paint, no squabbling over gossamer stuffs and shiny, impossible shoes.

We will not transgress again. We are even cycling together now, our menstruating bodies complying with what is preferred. We are one unit.

I seethe. Sleep will not come. I can hear Gosse speaking quietly to one of the Prefects outside the door, which is slightly ajar. The moonlight is bright tonight. I can even make out the particular shape of her shadow thrown across the slice of light on the floor—her beaky nose, long body, and short legs.

I sit up and notice that Ryan, who lies beside me, is awake. The whites of her eyes gleam but she does not move. She just lies there, looking at me. I will her to start talking to me but they are so strict with us now. They deprive us of a meal at the slightest excuse, make us chop wood for hours or clean the latrines for the whole compound. Yesterday after supper in the hour before Inspection, one of the Prefects strode across the room and made Walsh hold out her hands, palms upturned, for a whipping, just as though she were a girl-child. I don't even know what she had done.

They especially hate any whispering, even though they themselves have been whispering a great deal about the found objects in the lost Gated Community. They may be preoccupied but their eyes are on us at all times. And I have Gosse as well, shadowing me, talking in my ear, watching my every move.

Ryan still lies there looking almost pleadingly into my face. Her mouth moves silently, and I lean in to see if I can catch what she is trying to say. Her tongue and teeth glisten; she is trying to say the word *Laing*.

"Is she still here? Is she alive?"

Ryan rolls onto her back and stares up at the ceiling, then closes her eyes.

"Where is she?" I say it as close to her ear as I can. She clutches at my hand, then drops it.

"Is she here? After the Shearing, what did they

do?" I fear they have already taken her away for impregnation. "Did you see them take her back into the Darkness?"

She barely has time to nod before Gosse steps into the Dormitory.

Laing is still alive, I know it. And she is here.

CHAPTER SIXTEEN

THE DAYS PASS and the air becomes crisp. The big find, the cleansing, the imminent departure of the Committee Members all combine to make the community purposeful and busy. The larders are full. The Housekeepers are bottling preserves and making jams from the orchard fruit, the livestock have hay and grain, and the chickens are laying once again. The wind is bringing in cold clouds from the north. Soon this vault of blue air above will turn leaden. I think I smell snow in those clouds.

Everyone is happy but I am indifferent. A melancholy is upon me and I do not trust anything any longer. From what I can see, the earth tilts and moves differently now to a rhythm that we do not know nor can we predict.

Tonight everything changes. The wind has risen and is sweeping everything into disorder. Even the frost patterns, so precise on the windowpane, have been scattered into fragments. I slip my hand under my pillow, something I like to do just before I go to sleep, but this time I touch something cold and hard. My fingers slowly explore the object. I look over to Gosse. During the many nights when I cannot sleep, I have studied her. Sometimes the pained expression on her face slips away and she is released from her worries, but at other times all her concern flurries across her countenance and she twitches helplessly. Tonight is one of the nights when she is peaceful.

I inch the object out from under my pillow. Frosted moonlight gleams for a moment upon the blade.

The knife fits my hand quite well. Now that the light is on it, I see that a piece of paper has been wedged into the seam where the blade meets the bone handle. A note! Shaking with eagerness, I unfurl it. There is no writing upon it—the paper is a signal in itself. It is one of the flimsy pieces of paper that Amos uses to make her cigarettes. There are no instructions, no guidance. It is all she can offer me. I must make up my own mind as to what I am to do with this gift, this weapon.

I can think of no other way out. I must act now.

The floorboards are cold on my bare feet as I carry my boots over to the door. Bayles is there on duty to-night and she is awake. How am I to get past her? She turns in her seat and stares at me but she says nothing.

I wait. There is something strange in her expression, as if she were expecting me. Then she inclines her head, the merest of nods. I must move quickly now. I have no more time to think about her. I wonder how many minutes she will give me before she raises the alarm. Had she delivered the knife? Was this her one last lovelorn favor to Laing?

I have no time to think of either her passion or her inevitable punishment. I pull on socks and boots and then regret putting on the boots at all, because the noise of my footfalls crunching on the frost is so loud that it frightens me. But the wind is high again, pulling away the noise I am making. I slip on a patch of ice and almost lose my balance. The knife in my pocket falls out, and for a moment I stare at it before snatching it up again and running for the next shadow.

The razor wire around the boxes of the Darkness is coated with rime that glints under the fleeting moon. The razor wire! I had not even considered it.

Shivering now against the beating wind, and hunched in the nearest shadow to the wire, I have no idea how I will get inside. The gates are padlocked with huge, heavy locks. I take out the knife but at once see that I am never going to be able to pick such sturdy locks. The gates are also topped with the wire. I don't know what else to do. Taking my coat, I throw it over a patch of wire, where it snags and flaps like washing laid out to dry on a bush. Fingers sticking to the frosted wire of the fence, I climb until I have reached the coat. Taking a deep breath, I arch my whole body and try to launch myself over the barbs that have already sliced the coat's thick wool.

At first I don't feel anything except a jarring pain in my spine as I land on the inside of the fence, but when I look down, my clothes are torn and blood is already seeping from a hundred small cuts on my arms and torso. I check my hands; I will need my hands. They are also cut, but not badly. Then something worse occurs to me. The knife! It is in the pocket of my coat, still caught on the barbs high above me. There is so little time now. The torn flesh begins to sting, as if it has only just realized that it has been razored open. Still shaking, I nevertheless climb up the hard panels of wire and attempt to pull down at least some portion of my coat. I tug and tug. Frustration blazes inside me and I realize that I am now sobbing openly. There is the noise of ripping cloth as I pull away the side of my coat. I reach in and grab the knife, then drop to the ground sobbing and shivering, useless to all and anyone. I don't know how long I huddle there but the wind dies back and in the distance I hear a cock crow. Thoughts of impending daylight force me up and onward.

The boxes of the Darkness are pocked with rust. They have windows covered with iron grilles, but the windows are too small to climb through. Which box is she in? There is nothing for it but to pick the first one and work my way down the line. The doors of the boxes are held shut by chains fastened with locks. But these locks are fragile and old—they must think that there is no need for strong locks on the actual boxes. The ones inside are too weak to break free. They would never dare. And no one would ever try to break in, either. The Darkness causes such terror in us that no one else would ever come here willingly. Keeping my hands as steady as possible, I insert the knife and start to pick at the lock.

My hands hurt with cold but the pain of the cuts on my body seems, for the moment, to have disappeared. At last the mechanism releases and I push at the door. The room within is empty, nothing there but the smell of urine and despair. I have no other choice but to go from box to box. At least I get quicker at picking the locks, but it is only by the time I have reached the fourth box and look inside that I see a shape in the far corner, slumped on the bare floor. There is nothing else in the box, not a bed, not a latrine, nothing.

"Laing," I call. My breath hangs in little clouds on the dank air. "Laing."

There is no response. Perhaps she is dead already. I creep over and crouch down next to her. She is lying on her side, her head resting on her arm. Her fingers are curled around some object but it is difficult to see what it is.

"Laing, can you hear me?"

I am too overcome to say any more. As my eyes adjust to the weak light that spills from the single barred window, I am appalled by what I see of her.

Her legs, which are bare, are covered with sores. She is almost completely naked and she is spectrally thin. They must be starving her. I put my hand on her cheek; her skin feels cold, as though she were already dead.

"Laing," I whisper. Hot tears drop from my cheeks onto her cold face. "Laing, are you dead?"

But I know she is not because under my hand I can feel her rib cage rising and falling, shallow, dying breaths. She will not last until morning. And if she does, she will be impregnated. Or given away.

She needs warmth. Surely they must have given her a blanket or something. But all I can see as I grope around the floor are the last things she wore, her warrior shoes, a glint of gold from the underwear-like garments. And then I see the transparent coat, the one that was made of the strangest fabric, in a twisted heap in the corner. I lie down next to her and put my arms around her, try to warm her as best I can. Her fingers tighten and release for a second on the object she is trying to hold on to. It is some kind of paper cylinder. The most peculiar thing about the object is that when it moved in her fingers, it twinkled, even in this weak light. I lean over and take it from her loose fingers and then hold her as close as I can. It is like trying to warm a dying bird. I lie there listening to each tiny, desperate breath. Some of the blood from my own cuts is now on her. I try to wipe it away and her eyes, for an instant, flutter open.

Does she see me? Does she know that it's me?

I DON'T KNOW when I decide to do it. I don't even know how long I lie beside her. All I know is when I put the transparent coat made of that strange, airless material over her face and press it down and hold it there, she doesn't even struggle.

It does not take long.

I LEAN AGAINST one of the walls of the box, empty of everything.

Her hand is in mine. "We were betrayed," I say. "You and me. All of us."

I let her hand go and touch her cheek, which is still wet from my tears, but those tears have stopped now. I am talking to a dead body. Perhaps they were right about weeping: Tears will not help me at all.

My mind becomes blank. After some time of just sitting and staring at nothing, I remember the odd piece of paper that I took from her. In order to inspect it, I have to flatten it out. One sheet has been folded in two, the paper thicker than the paper of the slender books or the pages in the Library. It is creased and softened by time in the same way. Thin gray light slants through the window. By holding the paper object this way and that, it is possible to pick up the peculiar sparkles on its surface, and there are colored shapes on it. The surface of it beneath my fingers is abrasive, like touching frost, except without any sensation of cold. There are images upon it, cascades of pink blossoms falling and floating upon ripples of tinted water. The object must be something that Laing stole from Dayna's Room. *Happy Birthday, Darling Daughter,* it says in looping purple letters that also gleam a little. When folded out, there is another line of the gleaming writing: *A daughter is a gift whose worth cannot be measured except by the heart.* More glittering flowers and some butterflies fall through the air around the letters. There is also some handwriting in ink that may once have been dark but has faded to almost no color at all: *To our darling, special Dayna, Happy Birthday! We love you so much, more than words can say. Mom and Dad.*

What is *Dad*?

I read it one more time, running my fingers over the shining writing. Each letter is raised from the surface of the paper, like a welt. I trace the word *Birthday*—what could it mean? With all the blossoms and butterflies, it can't have anything to do with birth, of that I am certain. I fold the paper and put it in my pocket. The light outside is changing, lifting from gray to pale gold.

A cock crows. It is too late to escape.

THERE IS TOO much light. Like a belated warning, the cock crows a second time. I will be seen, but there is nothing I can do about it. I must run—but where? Will Amos or Smith find me? And if they do, what then? With a heavy sense of the inevitable, I see Gosse hurrying through the early dawn toward the padlocked gates, her limp ever more pronounced. She is alone, as I guessed she would be. If she reveals that she cannot guard me, then, with yet another failure to mark her, there will never be another chance at preferment. She needs this secrecy as much as I do.

From her belt she takes a key, unlocks the padlock, and slips into the enclosure. She calls out my name softly. Her voice is persuasive, like someone looking for a lost and frightened animal, one that they wish to feed and take care of until they kill it and eat it.

She comes closer, so I ready myself. I wait until she takes two steps closer and then I pounce. Her body is against mine; my arm is around her neck and her feet are suspended above the ground. She kicks a few times but compared to me she has little strength. Still, she does struggle and together the two of us grapple in all the strange intimacy of violence. I grab a handful of her hair and pull her up higher so that I can put the knife to her long, gulping throat. She starts to speak:

"Keller." She sounds calm, as if she is already defeated. "If you put the knife down, I can get you out of this. We can take your coat off the razor wire. No one will know."

For a moment I feel terrible pity for her, my guardian offering me my own survival in return for hers. I must remember what they have done to Laing.

"Stay away from me. Get away from me." It's more of a snarl. "You knew what they were going to do to Laing. Strap her up and impregnate her. And when they were finished, leave her to die or hand her over to someone beyond our borders to ravage as they pleased. You knew all along."

"You are wasting your time," pleads Gosse. "Let me go and we can keep this secret together. No one will ever know that you escaped from my protection."

My body is pressed so close to hers that the blood from my cuts is already sticky on her clothes. I can smell her, the sad, fish-meal smell, her failed smell. Her voice is tightening now because I have begun to press the knife harder to the tender skin between the ligaments of her neck. For a moment I wonder how tough the ligaments would be to cut. Would they spring apart as the flesh opens, or would they resist the knife with some terrible sinewy strength? Would it be as easy as slitting the throat of a rabbit, or something more effortful? Time seems to have slowed, but there is a slice of light on the horizon. When I see it, I know it is the end.

The failure that I can smell is my own. I could not release Laing in time. She could not come with me. I lower the knife.

"Get away from me," I say. "I will never, ever share a secret with you."

We stand facing each other, both panting. Our breath hangs before us on the cold air. She holds out her hand and then lets it drop helplessly.

Then I run. She makes no attempt to follow me. She stands there as I race down the slope. She knows I will be caught very soon.

The cock crows a third time and I am in the forest, dark, mist-filled, and quiet. I don't think I can run much farther. I know what I am running from, but I don't know what I am running toward.

CHAPTER SEVENTEEN

There is no light but it is not the Darkness.

There is no smell of rust, no clanking of chains. It must be a different prison, then. Someone has dressed my wounds. I lie and wait to hear the voice of Ms. Windsor. In my empty heart I know what I have done will make her want me even more. She will have viewed the body. She will know what I have done. She will have narrowed her eyes and hissed a command. "Find her." She thinks me ruthless. Everything I do confirms for her the rightness of her choice.

There are two shapes in the dark. One of the shapes is small. There is the flare of a match and the sting of smoke on the air.

"She's come around," says Amos. She draws on the cigarette again. The tiny point of light glows with the life of her breath. The other shape, Smith, gets to her feet. I reach out then, my hand waving about in the empty air, desperate to touch her. She holds my hand for a moment, then says, "Are you thirsty?"

My throat is parched but I am too weak to drink much, and soon I fall asleep again.

I FEEL as though I have slept for weeks. Perhaps I have, because I have lost all sense of time. The pain in my chest from running is the last thing I remember.

"Where am I? How long have I been here?"

"Just two nights." It is Smith who answers. "You're not the only one with a secret hideaway."

"Amos is a traitor," I say. "She meets with the enemy on beaches and takes tobacco from them." My voice is weak, as if coming from very far away. I am almost as exhausted now as I was when I dropped in the forest.

Amos gives a little rasping sigh that is full of impatience.

"Where the hell do you think things come from? We trade with them. Of course we do. Tea. Tobacco. Matches. Pepper. Fur. Honey. They even give us the honeybees. Where did you think all those essential things came from? We don't make them and we need them." With her yellowed fingers, she picks a strand of tobacco from her tongue. She is close enough for me to see a vein pulsing on her hairless scalp.

"All the talk, all the stuff we make you do, the Trackers, the guarding. The fear of invasion. It's all become a kind of game. No one is invading anyone." She looks up at me, the familiar anger in her amber eyes. "But if you want to keep your power, you must invent an enemy."

"*I* didn't invent them," I say bitterly. Something gives me the courage to answer her back. "And if they are not the enemy, then who are they? What were you doing with them on the beach that night?"

"Yes, well, I underestimated you. I should never have allowed that walkabout. I knew there was a chance you might come across the trade that was soon to happen. But we have to wait for the right conditions—fog, no moon, calm sea—and then we have to do it. And that night was the night. We only just avoided getting caught ourselves, by the Trackers who still serve her."

"You mean there are some Trackers who are loyal and some who are not?"

"Most are loyal. They still believe what is told to them."

"But if we need these things, why can't we just trade with these men out in the open?"

"Ms. Windsor would never allow it. She needs to keep her own system in place. She finds them disgusting. She believes that if we are seen touching them, even breathing the same air as they breathe, then our purity is violated. She wishes that the trade need not exist at all and pretends it does not. And they are a threat to her absolute power. We are women alone. That is who we are and have always been. That is her belief, and the bedrock of her power."

"Does the Headmistress know?"

"Yes."

"What do we give them in return?"

"Found objects, for the most part. Sometimes nothing. Sometimes they give us gifts."

"It's trade they want, not war," says Smith. "There are many among us who don't realize how much contact we have, but there are also many who have begun to suspect."

I try to sit up so that I can see her face better, but I cannot. After she has given me water, she too rolls and lights a cigarette. As the match flame flares, I see that we are deep under the ground in a kind of hole or tunnel that has walls and floors made of beaten earth. There are rough beams above and there is a rope ladder to a trapdoor. A few essential supplies are laid out: blankets, a drum with a spigot from which Smith drew the water, and an oil lamp.

"If the Headmistress knows, then surely Ms. Windsor must know that you trade with them," I say.

"She knows and she does not know," Smith says. "She still doesn't know exactly who in our community is doing it, but what we do is, in one way, very useful. We all need these things. But in another way the trading also undermines her power. So she lets it go on, but when she feels it is a threat, she finds someone to punish, someone to hold up as an example and to strike fear in the hearts of anyone else who contemplates disobeying the rule of the land. When she is finished with that, she will let it quietly continue for as long as it suits her. Then there will be another purge. That's the way it works." Smith shrugs. "It's just the way of things."

For a sudden sickening moment I imagine Ms. Windsor just above us, wrapped in fur, flying over the ground hither and thither, the energy of her search searing the very ground beneath her.

"The snakes," I mutter. "She said I saw a snake. She says I have the seeing eye."

Smith holds up her hand to stop Amos from speaking. Feebly I reach out to hold it. She shifts over to me and I topple sideways into her lap. She strokes my hair.

"It is part of her madness," she says. "She is in so much agony that it is turning her insane. The white powder that kills her pain gives her visions. She thinks she can see snakes everywhere. She thinks that if you saw one and resisted it, it means you are the one to succeed her. The snake is a sign that her dominion is threatened."

"She sells us," I say. "That is what happens to the girls who go away sometimes and never come back. She told me. She didn't call it selling but that is what it is. She calls it 'giving away.' But that's how she gets the powder. She was going to impregnate Laing, and if she survived the birth, Ms. Windsor was going to sell her."

Even in the gloom I can see that Smith blanches. She looks at Amos and her voice wavers. "The disappeared ones . . . no one knew where they went, not us, not even the Headmistress."

"Laing is gone." I feel as if my heart were being cleaved in two.

"They took her?"

"No. I did it. She is gone."

Smith closes her eyes and continues to stroke my hair and we remain like this for a long while. Then she holds the cup of water to my lips.

"Why are you protecting me?" I sound bleak and small—and angry. "If Ms. Windsor finds me, she will impregnate me or have me given away."

"Ms. Windsor has become obsessed with you. She thinks she owns you and you could end up spending a lifetime in servitude to her. You would have no access to the outside world other than the access she grants you. There would be no kind of freedom at all. She would control you and turn you into the same crazed creature that she is." Even Amos sounds panicked. "We could not save Laing and we could not save Carrow, but we have a chance to save you."

"How, how will you save me? You have no real

power." I am amazed at the reserves of savage anger that flames in everything I am saying to them. "She will punish you too. There will be Silent Beatings and then you will be sent to the Darkness."

"Perhaps," concedes Amos. "Then again, we have outwitted her so far."

"She may even sell you."

At this they burst out into rueful laughter. "I doubt it," says Smith. "We're far too old—and ugly. They only want the young ones, the perfect ones."

"This pain she has must mean she is ill. Is she dying?"

"She has some disease, it is true, but she has an extraordinary will to live, a will to power. She burns for it."

They exchange looks. "We must send you beyond the borders. It is the only choice."

"But it may not be what I want to do." I sound petulant as well as exhausted. "I am sick of only choices, and anyway, what do you know of those places? They are the parts unknown. And how can I trust you? I'm not going."

"Stop talking. You should rest." When Amos says this, something inside me explodes and releases a dark, hot stream of anger.

"Stop talking? I will not! I have things to tell *you*! *You* sit there and shut up! *You* listen to me!" Amos blinks and Smith tries to say something but I cut her off. "Don't speak! Don't say a single word! I will tell you this: I will tell you that you ordered us around all our lives and told us how we had to behave, and what was best for us, and what we had to do, and all the while you yourselves weren't doing any of it! No, you were off meeting up with the enemy on beaches, laughing and drinking and trading goods. And they weren't even the enemy! All that stupid training for nothing. You *lied* to us! You told us found objects were toxic and they're not, are they? You told us about Pitfalls—ha! Pitfalls! You set standards that you yourselves didn't keep—you just expected us to keep them." Amos is staring at me, aghast, but I care nothing for what she thinks or may do to me. "You're all the same! You want to know what you are?" Sweat is pouring down my face but I feel no pain, no fatigue; I feel as though I am flying, powered by this dizzying rage. "Do you want to know what you are?" I bellow the words. I don't care if the whole world hears. Smith and Amos sit, their backs pressed up against the wall, a look of shock on their faces. "You're weak!" I scream. "You're liars and hypocrites! You're all full of it! You and your community—it's a crock of shit!"

I AM so weary of darkness. Hours of silence have followed my outburst. I don't know what the time is and I have no idea if there is daylight above or not. After the exhilaration of my temper tantrum, I feel empty and sad. I didn't even mean half of what I said anyhow. Smith and Amos have risked their lives to save me and I screamed at them that they were liars, that they were weak—and they are not. And I loved learning to ride and shoot. And I was proud of our community.

And yet I did mean what I said.

Smith is sitting in the corner, dozing, I think. I creep over and curl up next to her. She puts her arm around me and I put my head in her lap. She smooths my hair as I sob. A terrible, hauling grief wrenches my heart. *Crybaby,* I tell myself, *big, fat crybaby*. But it does not make me stop. At length, as the weeping subsides, Smith says, "Let me tell you a story."

Amos, who had been sitting with her back to me smoking morosely into the air vent, turns around and shuffles in a little closer.

"It began long ago," says Smith. "We were young Trackers. Things were different, better than they are now. There was so much hope. It was a time when we believed in what we were told by our leaders. We loved our work and it was what we knew. We were loyal to our community and to all the women who worked together to help one another survive and find meaning. But then this thing happened to us and we couldn't seem to stop it.

"One night a small group of men washed ashore.

Their vessel was in pieces. We caught them but we were terrified; we had no idea what to do with them. We were so young and so curious. And then we saw that they were more frightened of us than we were of them. Later they told us that we were legend. They called this place 'Nomansland,' and apparently on all the maps that we have never seen, that is the name of what we call Foundland. They said that all who live beyond our borders think we are cannibals, which means people who eat human flesh. They say we crave the flesh of young men, whom we keep in cages and whom we cook and eat in elaborate ceremonies. I'm not sure they believed us when we laughed and said they were too skinny to eat.

"Two of them were injured and the third one *was* skinny. They were frightened of us. We wanted them to stay and in the end we did put them in a cage. They were astounded at how quickly we made one. But they were terrified too. As they watched us lashing branches together they looked kind of gloomy!"

Smith starts to laugh and ends up coughing so hard that Amos has to get her some water.

"It didn't need to be a particularly strong cage," she continues, "because they were so weak. They had been without food and water for many days. In the beginning they just hunched up and sulked, even refusing food at first. But after a while, things changed. The weather was warm and we were on our first free tour of duty."

Smith chuckles. "We couldn't take our eyes off them. Surprisingly they spoke to us in our language. We understood them with ease. When they started to eat, they talked a bit more. And we had to do something about their wounds—wounds which, by the way, we had inflicted. They're terrible babies about pain. But we were so fascinated by them, by their voices and the different ways in which they moved. They made us laugh. They told us about their land, about the different things they do, like make ocean-going vessels that burn oil and are propelled by engines. They told us that they can grow tobacco, and they told us how they live together with women. They have congress with them and, of course, produce children. The way they described things was confusing. It never sounded as if there were any order in that place, just a kind of mess of people—men, women, and children here and there—although I suppose to them it must have seemed to make more sense."

Here she pauses and sips some water. "All their children are mutants," she says, wiping her mouth. "Many of them die before their fifth year. In fact, we think that nearly all of them, the adults too, are deviants, imperfect and deformed. Not pure like us.

These three that we had in the cage had deformities, but not the kind that hampered them in their work, which was to find other lands to trade with. It is they who brought the tobacco and showed us how to make cigarettes. They brought the grain spirit they drink, which we drink too from time to time. They have a name for the drink, which is 'moonshine,' but they do not know why it is called this, or perhaps they have just forgotten in the same way we have forgotten why we do so many of the things we do.

"Well, anyway, we kept them in the cage for many days but in the end, when their injuries were somewhat healed, we released them. They stayed around, though, and we even helped them patch up their vessel. Then they set sail."

"But they came back?"

"Yes," said Amos flatly. "They came back."

"Why?" I know the answer but I want to hear her say it.

There is a long silence. It is really going to cost her.

"Because I fell in love with one of them," she says. "The one you saw that night. I love him." She looks at me, her expression both defiant and tender, and shrugs. "That's what you wanted to hear me say, isn't it?"

"Did you . . . do you . . . have congress with him?"

She gives me a grin and a look like the one she gave me the day she joked about her cigarette smoking. "None of your business."

"Why don't you go back with him to his land?" And this time the pause is even longer.

"Because I'm scared," she says at last. "I can't do it."

I can't believe my ears. *Amos*? *Scared*? She gives me another of her rare crooked smiles but does not elaborate.

"Do they beat and rape their women? Do they make them their slaves?" All this topsy-turvy information—Smith and Amos and their secret lives, their secret weaknesses. I want to sleep now and my wounds have begun to ache, but I need to know everything.

Smith sees how pale my face has become. "Lie down," she says. "Sip your water."

"What do they do to the women?" I insist. "Do their women serve them?"

"We don't know. It's not that straightforward. They tell us so many things that contradict each other. It's not perfect. But the women there work and when they have children, even though they are mutants, they keep them and love them and look after them. And the men who father them love them too. That is what they tell us. The men travel and trade. They are away for long periods of time and the women take care of everything, but then the men come back from time to time."

Smith gazes off into the dark beyond our small circle of light. "I don't know, Keller, I just don't know. In the long run it may be that what men mostly do to women . . ." She hesitates, feeling her way into her thought. "Is make them feel lonely."

"But you say they love their children, even the mutant ones."

"That is what they tell us. They love their children differently."

"Differently? Different from the way . . ." I don't know how to finish what I have started to say. "So if I go, it's just a leap in the dark. I must trust you—and them."

"Yes," she says. "But most of all you must trust yourself. It must be your decision. We cannot force you to go."

WE SPEND what seems like endless nights in the hole. There is no telling when it is day or night. At intervals Amos clambers up the ladder and disappears.

"There are search parties everywhere. Trackers loyal to us have reported that Ms. Windsor wants you back, that you belong to her. The Trackers who are working for us have made false trails so that she thinks you have gone to the interior," says Smith.

Some of my wounds have become infected and I have a fever. The hours unspool into this small, smoky space of nothingness below the ground, another place where no one can hear me cry out.

Smith remains by my side, tipping water into my mouth and rubbing some kind of ointment upon the cuts. The ointment smells of herbs, of the mint and oregano that we grow when the weather is kind and the vegetable garden turns green. It is only then that we are absolved of the sins of the past because the plants are proof of our penance and our renewed bond with the earth. At last my fever breaks and I gain strength.

Smith waits until I am a little restored, then she tells me: "We are falling apart, Keller. The Seed is dwindling. Our crop is worse with each cycle. We must change or die out completely." She covers her face with her hands. "We can no longer sustain this isolation."

The trapdoor opens and Amos drops down into the space. She looks exhausted, too exhausted even to smoke. "The search party has moved toward the interior. If we are to move, we have to do it now."

Like a girl-child, I clutch at Smith. To my astonishment, I see tears start to roll down her lined cheeks.

"Come with me. Please." I am so scared. Smith turns to Amos and says, "She could stay . . . live with us in hiding . . . or one of us could go with her."

Amos bites her lip and looks down. "There may be others whom we have to get out to safety. It is the only useful thing we can do until . . ."

"Until what?" I don't really want to hear the answer.

"Until we die," says Amos. "We are sick." She is trying to sound matter-of-fact but her voice breaks. "We can't be sure but we think it is the tobacco."

As she speaks she is rolling a cigarette. "The tobacco," she says, seemingly lost in thought as the blue smoke drifts up into the air around her.

"So we never really needed tobacco, did we? You said it was essential, but it wasn't, was it?" I sound accusing, and then when I see her face I regret what I have said.

"We're not perfect, Keller," she says. And after she has answered me, she just looks broken and sad.

"Where will you and Smith go?"

"Into hiding," she says curtly. She keeps looking at Smith, as if Smith's tears are just as painful to her. "We both will. There are others who work with us. It is not just us. Ms. Windsor doesn't yet know the full extent of it, but she suspects. Why do you think she and the Committee Members stayed here so long? You weren't the only ones being watched."

Smith has stopped crying now. She begins to pack a water bottle and the lamp into a sack. She picks up my boots and motions for me to get up. Her face is half in shadow.

"An idea, a strong vision," she says. "A single idea, a narrow intent, is not enough to hold so many unique lives together. It started out . . ." Her whole being seems to sag but she starts again. "We had such purpose and now . . . I don't know. I think somewhere, somehow, we've gone wrong."

"I have an answer for you." I pause for a moment because I am not so sure of this answer as I sound.

"An answer for what?"

"For the question you asked me. Do I think a woman invented the wheel?"

She chuckles. "Ah, that question. So what's your answer?"

"It's no one person, either woman or man, inventing the wheel. It's the other way around. There's a wheel of invention. It goes around and around and no single person turns it. And as to how it turns, well, it is a mystery."

She touches my cheek with her finger. "Have you made your decision?"

I reach into my pocket where the folded paper is hidden. With my thumb I can feel its strange, frosted surface. *Happy Birthday, Darling Daughter. A daughter is a gift whose worth cannot be measured except by the heart.*

I have decided. I cannot live here any longer and I must find some other place that I can accept, and where they can accept me. I have seen what I have seen and I am no longer of this place. Something, some belief, has fallen away—something that will never return.

THE WAVES rock and spill on the shore. It is bitter cold and there is something new on the surface of the ocean: chunks of sea ice bobbing in toward the beach. There is no moon but the night is clear. We have seen the vessel's light only once and then it vanished. There is no wind, just biting cold and the sound of the sea. I touch my forehead awaiting the throbbing pain behind my eye, but there is no pain. My thoughts are as clear and cold as the water before me.

Amos and Smith stand beside me, scanning the dark water. As I look out I think, what if Laing could be here? She could rise from the waves, radiant in her golden garments, her wet hair twisted around her naked body, her warrior shoes. She would have white wings at her back and she would move toward me to brush my face with a feathered wing tip, like the last beautiful creature to emerge from the box in the story on the pages I once found.

But Laing does not rise from the waves.

A light flickers on, off, on again as the hulking vessel comes into view.

"Go," whispers Smith. She pushes me into the water. The surge of the undertow tugs at my legs and for a moment I want to succumb, to yield to its pull. And then the vessel is almost on top of me, reeking and huge. A figure bends over the side, a pair of work-hardened hands is offered, and as I clasp them, there is a shock: hair on the backs of the hands!

They drag me up against wet wood. There is the smell of tobacco. I can hear a number of unfamiliar voices, and the choice to surrender is no longer mine. I lie in a heap on the wet boards. Someone puts a gentle hand on my back.

"You'll be coming to live with us now, my dear." The voice is deep but rich with strange inflection. It makes me think of sun-warmed stone, a shaft of honey-colored light upon a wall. I can hear Smith saying, *They tell us that they look after their own children. They love their children differently*. I try to pick myself up and the owner of the voice helps me to my feet.

"You must be frozen to the bone," he says. When I look at him, I recognize him. It is the man whom Amos loves. He looms over me, his hideous long limbs dangling from the hump of his body.

"You'll catch your death," he says. "Come in where it's warm." He tries to take my hand but I pull away and turn to look back across the sea and the silent cliffs.

The puttering sound that I once heard so long ago begins. I lean into the frozen, moonless night and search the little beach.

No one is there.

ACKNOWLEDGMENTS

I am ever grateful to my agent, Ann Tobias, for fishing me out of the slush pile and for her amazing work on the manuscript. Thank you also to all the staff at Henry Holt Books for Young Readers for their enthusiasm and support, most especially my gifted editor, Sally Doherty. I am indebted to Sarah Manson for her crucial questions that were instrumental in shaping the story; Agnes Krup for being so generous with her precious time; and Jody Hotchkiss for his kind words. Thank you to Natasha Appleweis, Sarah Nazimova-Baum, and Arne Vaagen, who read the manuscript in its early stages; and to my friend and photographer, Sarah Pring. Heartfelt everything to my beloved family: the memory of Paul; my parents; my sons, Max and Leo. And Arild—I could not have done it without you.

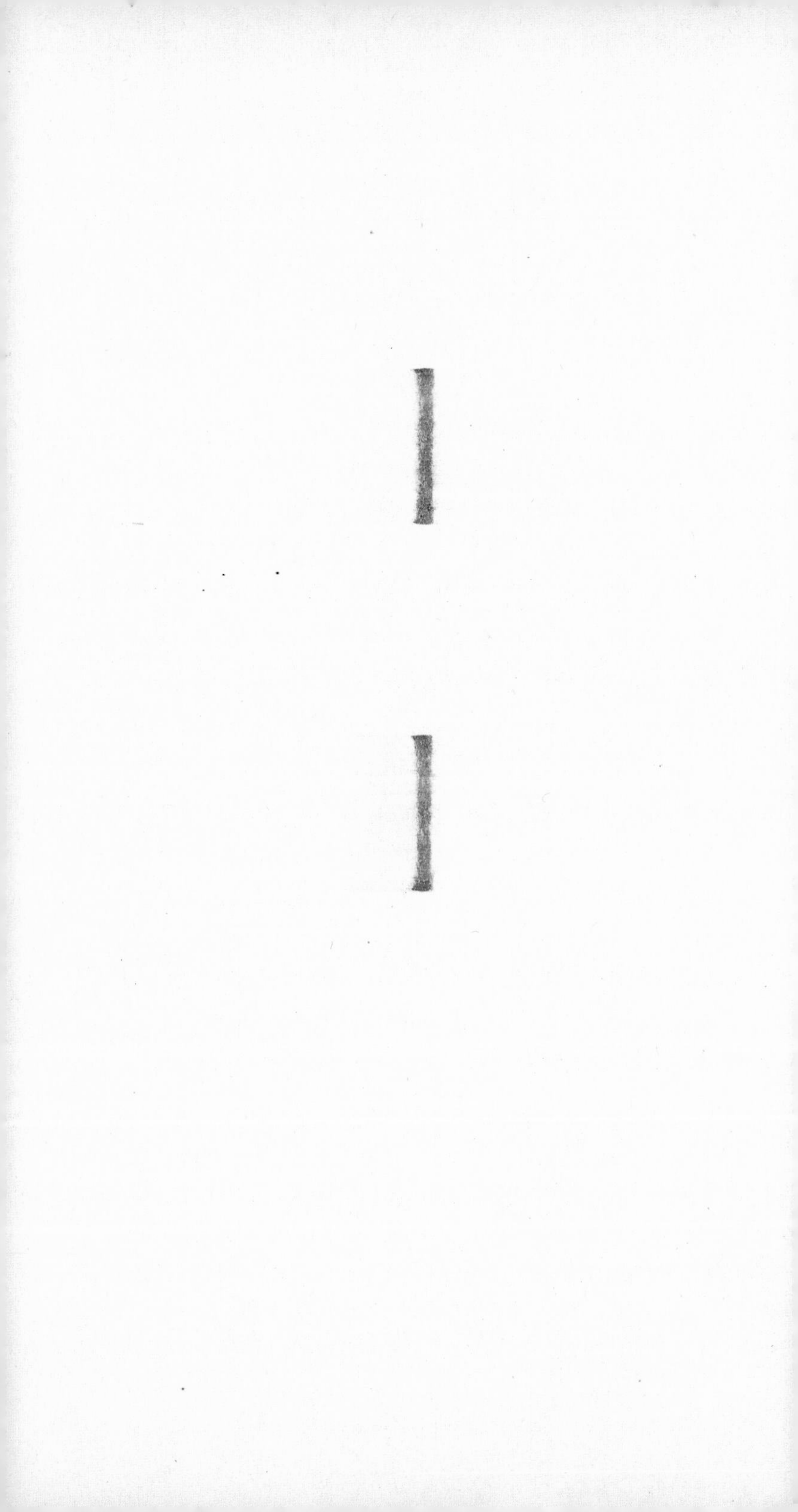